The thrill of t

Patrick Hazard had taken
Hester by surprise. She
falling in love with anyone, but Patrick wasn't
content just to be friends—he wined and dined
Hester, pursued her and wooed her, whatever it
took to win her over.

Secretly, Hester didn't need moonlight and
roses to tell her that she and Patrick shared
something special. As far as she was concerned,
now she was spoken for—or had she spoken
too soon? Patrick was a skilled campaigner and
he was offering her everything her heart
desired. Everything, that was, except marriage.

Catherine George was born in Wales, and early on developed a passion for reading which eventually fuelled her compulsion to write. Marriage to an engineer led to nine years in Brazil, but on his later travels the education of her son and daughter kept her in the UK. And instead of constant reading to pass her lonely evenings she began to write the first of her romantic novels. When not writing and reading she loves to cook, listen to opera, browse in antiques shops and walk the Labrador.

Recent titles by the same author:

NO MORE SECRETS
LIVING NEXT DOOR TO ALEX
THE SECOND BRIDE
BARGAINING WITH THE BOSS

THE COURTING CAMPAIGN

BY
CATHERINE GEORGE

MILLS & BOON®

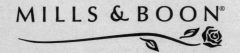

With grateful thanks to Beverley,
a very helpful, charming magistrate

*First published in Great Britain 1997
Harlequin Mills & Boon Limited,
Eton House, 18-24 Paradise Road, Richmond, Surrey TW9 1SR*

© Catherine George 1997

ISBN 0 263 80462 3

*Set in Times Roman 11 on 12 pt.
02-9711-46608 C1*

*Printed and bound in Great Britain
by Mackays of Chatham PLC, Chatham*

CHAPTER ONE

IT WAS the slight bow to the bench which caught Hester's attention. The man was a stranger—tallish, slim, wearing the kind of baggy tweed jacket which could have been Armani or Oxfam. Probably the former, she thought, glad that the next case was the last of the session. The courtroom was hot. June sunshine blazed down from high windows onto a newly refurbished decor of cream-painted walls, crimson tip-up seats and flowered curtains—very different from the old, beautiful oak-panelling of pre-refit days. Now the entire courthouse was light and bright, but lacked its former *gravitas*. There was nothing here to intimidate the offenders brought up before the magistrates, most of whom, like Hester Conway, felt nostalgia for the courtroom in all its previous Victorian splendour.

So far the morning had provided the usual quota of summary offences involving traffic, excess alcohol and breaches of the peace, and the sentences had been straightforward. Hester was a relatively new magistrate, and at thirty-four the youngest in the district. In consequence she tended to dress down for her days in court. Despite the heat of the day her suit was unrelieved navy, and her dark hair was caught back in a severe twist with no escaping wisps. A large pair of horn-rimmed spectacles provided the finishing touch for the role she took very seriously. On her mettle to prove she possessed the intelligence, common sense, integrity and fair play required of her as a lay magistrate, she had, as usual, paid meticulous attention to every shred of evidence presented during the morning by both prosecution and defence. Today the three magistrates consisted of herself, Dr Tom Meadows—senior partner of the local medical practice—and Mr Philip Galbraith—retired headmaster of the local boys' school, and President of the Bench.

Before the break most of the defendants had pleaded guilty and accepted whatever penalties, compensation and fines had been handed out. But the defendant about to be tried was pleading not guilty, which meant a lengthier, contested session to round off the morning.

Hester noted a reporter from the local paper, plus a sprinkling of spectators in the seats provided, including the man in the tweed jacket, who stood out from the rest. She registered thick fair hair, a deep-dyed suntan, and a clear-cut cast of feature which combined good looks with intelligence. Attractive, she thought, returning to her notes.

'Who's the fair man at the back?' muttered Philip Galbraith, who always assumed Hester knew everyone in the entire neighbourhood.

'No idea,' she returned in an undertone. 'Ask Dr Meadows.'

But the doctor was no wiser.

'Dominic Anthony Barclay,' announced the usher, and a tall youth entered the court and took a seat in the last of the three rows in the body of the court.

'Stand up, Mr Barclay,' said the President without emphasis, and the boy shot to his feet.

Hester eyed him with interest. During the morning all the defendants, male and female, had been dressed with a certain uniformity. Gaudy sweatshirts, jeans, sneakers and multiple earrings on both male and female had been the order of the day. Dominic Anthony Barclay, however, was in grey flannel trousers, crisp white shirt, striped tie and navy blazer. His fair hair—instead of hanging down his back, cropped cruelly short or shaved off entirely—was expertly cut, allowing one shining lock to flop slightly over his forehead.

He gave his name and address in educated, accentless tones, and despite obvious nerves firmly stated his plea of not guilty to the offence of driving while disqualified.

When asked what had happened on the night in question he informed the bench that his brother had been driving his car.

He was allowed to sit down while the prosecution informed the bench that the defendant had been recognised at the wheel of a car by a policewoman on the night of March twenty-fourth in Ashdown Lane, six months after having been disqualified from driving for two years. The witness for the prosecution was WPC Jean Harding, the policewoman in question.

WPC Harding, a bright-eyed young woman in her mid-twenties, made a good impression in the witness box. She repeated her oath as firmly as the defendant, but with an attractive hint of local burr in her voice.

In response to the prosecution's enquiry she confirmed that she had been driving down Ashdown Lane on the night in question, just as it had been growing dark. There had been parked cars on both sides of the narrow road, and she had pulled in to a kerbside space to allow a current model Ford Escort to pass. She had recognised Dominic Barclay at the wheel. There had been another passenger in the defendant's vehicle, but in the few seconds necessary for the car to travel past she'd been certain only of the identity of the driver.

The young policewoman gave her evidence calmly, consulting her notebook where necessary, and Hester scribbled a few notes of her own on her pad. The prosecution went on to ask the policewoman how she knew the defendant, and learned that WPC Harding had been the officer who had attended Ashdown House two weeks earlier to request the defendant to turn down the volume of music at a party given there to celebrate his birthday.

'And on that occasion were you close enough to Mr Barclay to see his features clearly?'

'Yes,' continued the policewoman woodenly. 'He kissed me on both cheeks and invited me to join the party. When I declined he reduced the volume as requested, whereupon my colleague and I left the premises.'

The prosecution sat down, and the defending solicitor rose to his feet to ask if, on the night of the party, Mr Barclay's behaviour had been offensive.

'No,' said the policewoman.

'But he did kiss you and invite you to the party. Was there a reason for this?' asked the defendant's solicitor gently.

The girl coloured. 'He thought I was a stripper-gram,' she said, after a pause, and the solicitor smiled indulgently as a ripple of amusement ran through the court.

'Did this annoy you, Constable?'

'No, sir.'

'The incident did not prejudice you in any way when you believed you saw the defendant at the wheel of the Escort?'

The girl's mouth tightened. 'No, sir.'

'And during your visit to Ashdown House did you have occasion to meet Dominic Barclay's brother?'

'No, sir.'

'Thank you, Constable.'

Hester made more notes as the witness was excused. Young Dominic's guilt seemed cut and dried. Then a hush fell over the court as the usher showed a young man to the witness box.

Giles Edward Barclay gave his name and address, took the oath and stated that he was the brother of the defendant. The statement was unnecessary. Right down to the last shining hair he was a mirror image of Dominic. The Barclay brothers were identical twins.

In unemphatic tones the boy informed the bench that he had been driving the car on the night in question, due to his brother's disqualification.

Hester watched him closely as he gave his evidence. He looked nervous, in common with most youths of his age in these circumstances, but he answered the questions steadily enough, confirmed that he possessed a current driving licence and made a very good impression. Hester glanced at the man in the visitors' seats. He was sitting perfectly still, his eyes on the boy in the witness stand, no vestige of expression on his face. Yet Hester was sure that behind the imperturbable exterior the man was tense. He looked extraordinarily young to possess teenage sons, but the resemblance was unmistakable. He was obviously their father.

She returned her attention to the proceedings. After only the shortest of consultations between the three magistrates the case was dismissed, and Dominic

Barclay was told he was free to go—after a pointed reminder from the President that the term of disqualification from driving still had fifteen months to run.

'There was no way that we could prove that he, or his brother, was lying,' said Philip Galbraith later as they finished for the day. 'But I've had years of experience with boys like Dominic Barclay, not to mention the pranks played by identical twins.'

'You think the other boy lied?' asked Hester, collecting her belongings.

'If he did he was damn good,' said Dr Meadows. 'The Barclays are new in the district, by the way. Bought Ashdown House a few months ago. They're shelling out a small fortune on doing it up.'

'They haven't shelled any out at Conway's,' said Hester with regret.

'Shouldn't think they're straight yet. I went out to visit Mrs Barclay not long ago. The place was still a shambles.' The doctor looked at his watch. 'Must dash. Might get some lunch in before afternoon surgery.'

Hester made her farewells and went out into the sunshine. The small Cotswold town was full of visitors during the summer months, and on a sunny market day like this the streets were thronged. She exchanged her horn-rims for sunglasses, and walked briskly up the steep main thoroughfare. At the top of the hill she caught sight of the Barclay twins looking at sports equipment in a shop window, in company with their father. Relieved that the eye-catching Barclays were engrossed in the window display, Hester crossed the road to avoid an encounter likely to embarrass all of them—herself included.

She turned into the cobbled walkway where attractive shops clustered together near the medieval arches of the Chastlecombe market hall. At one end a glass-vaulted arcade housed vendors of expensive clothes and leather goods as well as a small restaurant, aromatic with the scent of freshly-brewed coffee. But in the cobbled square itself the name CONWAY in italic capitals, was emblazoned above a large premises which sold porcelain and furniture. Some of the latter was the better type of mass-produced product, but the pieces displayed in the windows were made by local craftsmen and drew customers nationwide.

The shop was full of customers, and Hester hurried through to the cloakroom at the back to change the navy wool jacket for a cool white blouse. On her way back into the shop she saw David Conway at the desk in the office, involved in a heated telephone argument. He grinned at her, pointed an imaginary gun at the phone and went on arguing. Hester grinned back, blew him a kiss and hurried off to relieve her beleaguered staff.

After the sale of some hand-painted plates, a David Conway sofa table and a small, exquisite Kilim rug, Hester assented with relief when David emerged from his workshop to suggest a late snack in the bar of the King's Arms.

While David went up to the bar Hester found a seat at a table near the window to watch the world go by, glad to relax for a while after the demands of the morning.

'Busy in court today?' asked David as he joined her.

'Fairly.' She accepted her tall glass of mineral water with gratitude, smiling at him, but the smile faded as she saw the father of the Barclay twins ushering his sons to a table. To her embarrassment he caught sight of her and bowed slightly, just as he'd done in court.

David raised an eyebrow. 'Someone you know?'

'Not really.'

The arrival of their sandwich lunches saved Hester from explanations, and the rest of the meal passed with discussion of the new commission David had been given that morning.

'A twelve-foot dining table, a dozen chairs, two sideboards and a credence table,' he said with satisfaction. 'The argument was over a delivery date. The lady seemed to think I could knock them up in a couple of weeks. If, I told her, she wants the hand-crafted perfection of all David Conway pieces, it will take a little bit longer than that. Even,' he added, 'with the invaluable Peter doing the pedestrian bits.''

Hester grinned. 'Is the customer happy about it?'

'Happy, no. Resigned, yes.'

'It's a big order to do in a hurry. You've got a lot of work on already, David,' said Hester anxiously.

'Can't afford to turn any away!' He reached out a hand and took hers. 'Don't worry, love. I'm as healthy as a horse. Honestly. Ask Tom Meadows.'

'I would, too,' she said tartly, 'but he'd never breach patient confidentiality.' She withdrew her hand to finish her drink. 'I'm still thirsty. I'd like some coffee. Want some?'

'No, thanks.' David rose to fetch it for her, but she waved him back.

'Stay there and finish your lunch. I'll get it.'

When Hester turned away from the bar with her coffee she realised the twins' father was watching her.

'A secret admirer?' teased David, when she got back to the table.

'He was in court this morning,' said Hester, and changed the subject to the new furniture commission.

All the while David was expounding on the design he intended for the new order, his dark eyes bright with his usual, irresistible enthusiasm, Hester said the right things in the right places but couldn't help noticing that the Barclay twins—who were in her direct line of vision on the other side of the bar—looked very subdued. Their father appeared to be giving them a lecture while they ate. Which wouldn't do them any harm, she thought, feeling far more sympathy for the other youngsters who'd been brought up before the bench that morning, all of whom could have done with some of the parental guidance the Barclay twins were receiving.

Hester brought herself up sharply, and concentrated on David. In her year of sitting on the bench she'd made it a strict rule to put the cases from her mind once she left the court.

'Come on, beautiful dreamer,' said David, downing the last of his lager. 'Time we got back to the grind.'

On their way out of the bar their route took them past the Barclays' table, where both boys looked embarrassed when they saw Hester. She smiled a little, managing not to look in their father's direction, and went out into the sunshine with David.

'Nice-looking lads,' he commented. 'Visitors, I suppose.'

'No. Their family moved into Ashdown House a few months ago.'

'How do you know them?' he asked curiously. 'Or shouldn't I ask?'

'That's right—you shouldn't.'

He grinned, then whistled in surprise as they found the shop full of tourists admiring the porcelain display Hester had taken such pains to arrange. 'Now you're back from your bench I'll get back to mine,' he said hurriedly, and left her to see to the welcome influx of customers with her usual friendly attention.

Hester enjoyed her side of the business. David was the creative artist, but she was a skilled buyer, a born saleswoman, and in her element when it came to dealing with the public. Conway's employed two women in their forties as assistants—Iris, who worked part-time, and Sheila, who worked full-time and did the accounts. The other employees were Mark, who was in his twenties and possessed of a physique which came in very useful for hauling furniture around and Peter, who assisted in the workshop. Mark also accompanied Ted Burrows, the driver, when deliveries were made in the smart van with CONWAY printed in gilt on a field of dark green.

Life for Hester Conway was busy and full, both professionally and socially. She went on regular visits to trade fairs all over the country, sometimes attended various functions with David—who was a Rotarian, and president of the local chamber of commerce—and when business was slacker in the post-Christmas lull holidays were spent in some warmer clime than the UK. She was also a member of the history society, the tennis club and contributed time to charity work, as well as attending regular additional periods of training for her unpaid function as a lay magistrate. Some days were so hectic that a few extra hours in the twenty-four would have been welcome.

As they shut up shop at five-thirty David reminded

her they were due at a wine-tasting party at Chastlecombe House at eight-thirty, in aid of the local children's home.

'I'm off to see Father first,' he said, looking at his watch. 'I'll go straight there, have supper with him at The Priory and meet you at the wine-tasting later.'

'Right. Give him my love and tell him I'll see him on Sunday.'

Robert Conway, David's father, had been the founder and driving force of the business, but twelve months earlier he'd decided to retire. He'd sold his house and acquired a room at The Priory, which was more like a five-star hotel than the luxurious retirement home it actually was. He still drove his car, visited Lords cricket ground once a year for a test match and went off on a cruise whenever the fancy took him. His family took turns in entertaining him at Sunday lunch every couple of weeks or so, and the arrangement worked well for everyone, since Robert still took a keen interest in the business and was only too glad to step in whenever Hester and David needed a break.

Hester lived on the outskirts of town. Pear Tree Cottage was small, but with a sizeable garden with high hedges which enclosed a riot of colour at this time of year. Hester ate a swift salad dinner then went through the nightly ritual of watering her latest batch of bedding plants, wishing she could just potter about in the garden all evening. She was tired after the double drain of a morning in court before the session in the shop. It was an effort to shower and change for the charity evening, where she would see the same familiar faces that she encountered at pretty much every function she attended in the close-knit community of Chastlecombe.

Chastlecombe House retained all the Cromwellian severity of its origins, both inside and out. Since Mrs Cowper, its owner, was very kind in lending it out for charity events Hester knew it well. By the time she arrived the great hall, with its long trestle-table and heavy, carved furniture, was crowded, but two faces new to the community stood out. One of them was already familiar from the morning session in court. The other was a rather haggard, attractive woman who, from the striking resemblance, could only be the Barclay twins' mother. And even from a distance it was easy to see that Mrs Barclay was pregnant.

'How charming you look in that shade, Hester,' said Mrs Cowper, emerging from the crowd to greet her. 'Used to call it dusky pink when I was a girl. You know everyone, dear, so do mingle. Though if you fancy making yourself useful we could use an extra hand to pass round the nibbles.'

Hester agreed with alacrity. She took up two beautiful silver dishes—George III, she noted with respect—and made for the nearest group with her canapés.

'Hester!' said Tim Galbraith, son of Philip. 'You look ravishing.'

To prevent his usual kiss Hester thrust the silver dishes at him, grinning. 'Hands off, Tim. Have one of these nibbles.'

'I'd rather nibble delectable you, Hester,' he assured her, relieved her of one of the dishes and accompanied her from group to group round the crowded room, flirting with her outrageously as they went.

Tim Galbraith ran the local garden centre. In sight of forty, he remained happily unmarried and was such a charmer that every single woman of eligible age chased him with fervour. To date he remained unattached but never neglected—since he wined and dined several of the ladies in question in strict rotation, never giving any of them reason to believe he cared for one more than another. Hester collected more supplies, then circulated, with Tim again in tandem. As they approached the Barclays Hester became gradually aware that the twins' father was watching her with something like disapproval.

She thrust her dish at Tim. 'Carry on for me, would you, please? I see David's car coming down the drive.'

'Only if you swear to return to me later.' He grinned. 'Or should I ask David's permission?'

The evening was pleasant, as always, and Chastlecombe House was a dramatic backdrop for the occasion, but Hester took pains to avoid meeting the newcomers. Mr Barclay would be bound to mention that she was a Justice of the Peace, which would be embarrassing for his wife, and it was with some relief that she saw them take leave of Mrs Cowper quite early. Because Mrs Barclay was pregnant, of course, thought Hester. And not overly young to be expecting a baby, either. The twins were eighteen, which presumably would put their mother in the forty-something age group, which was common enough these days—but the lady had looked very weary.

By the time David took Hester home she felt weary, too, and utterly lacking in enthusiasm for the following day, which was Saturday, and, in summer-season Chastlecombe, likely to be busy.

She was proved right. After a satisfying busy morning, Hester sent Iris and Sheila off to an early lunch, volunteering to hold the fort with only Mark for company until they got back.

'If necessary I'll lure Peter from the workshop,' she assured David, who wanted to go home for a while.

'I need to do some shopping on the way,' he told her. 'But if you get mobbed, ring me.'

There was usually a lull at this time on a Saturday, while shoppers went off in search of lunch in the many and various eating places in the town. Hester had no problem in coping with a group of polite Japanese tourists who spent a gratifying amount of money. Afterwards there were a few people looking rather than buying, then for a time the shop was empty. Mark kept watch while Hester brushed her hair and reapplied lipstick, then popped his head round the office door and told her someone was asking for her. Hester was prey to mixed feelings when she found the Barclay twins' father looking at dining room furniture.

He turned, smiling, as she went towards him. 'Good afternoon. I wondered if you could help me?'

She returned the smile politely. 'Of course, if I can.'

'I'm in need of a gift for my sister—a belated house-warming present. And while I'm here I'd like a desk. For myself,' he added. 'I have it on the best authority that I won't do better anywhere in the Cotswolds.'

'How gratifying. May I ask who told you that?'

'Mrs Cowper, at the wine-tasting last night. It was very good of her to invite us. And very informative,' he added, smiling. 'I learned a lot about the inhabitants of Chastlecombe.'

The day was hot and he was dressed for it, in pale

chinos and a thin cotton shirt with the sleeves rolled up. The shirt, Hester couldn't help noticing, was the exact silvery green of the eyes which were so arresting in his lean, sun-browned face.

'I must remember to thank Mrs Cowper,' she said pleasantly, glad she'd tidied herself up before he arrived. Nor was she in any position to criticise him for vanity—her own amber linen dress had been chosen to match the eyes she looked on as her best feature.

Hester looked at him enquiringly. 'What kind of gift do you have in mind?'

'I've no idea.' He gazed about him. 'The gilt-framed mirror over there. Surely that's old?'

'That's a commission piece; I occasionally provide a selling-on service for people who don't wish to advertise their valuables.' Hester took the mirror down carefully. The frame was old, the gilt almost greenish and the mirror itself quite murky. 'It came from a Venetian church. A friend at Sotheby's confirmed it as fifteenth century and suggested the price.'

He examined the discreet tag and raised an eyebrow, considered for a moment then nodded briskly. 'Right. A bit steep, but exactly what I want. Now I need a desk.'

Sheila reappeared at that point, leaving Hester free to take her customer upstairs to the showroom, where several desks were displayed in a corner decorated to suggest a study.

'Shall I leave you to browse?' she asked. 'All the desks are priced. You'll know best what you need.'

He eyed the array of desks with respect. 'I was informed that a David Conway piece would be an investment.'

'I agree, of course.'

He examined the ticket on a beautiful, simple desk crafted from yew. 'I see what you mean. This is obviously his work.'

'It is. And the two beyond are by other local craftsmen. The ones on this side are the usual reproduction type. Very good reproductions,' she added, 'but all alike. Each one of David's is unique. It depends on what you're prepared to spend. But please don't feel embarrassed if nothing here suits you.'

'I admit I hadn't intended being quite so extravagant,' he said thoughtfully, 'but, having met with a David Conway original, I realise what Mrs Cowper meant. It puts the others in the shade. Can you arrange to have it delivered?'

'Certainly. Monday morning, if you like.'

'Perfect. At the moment I'm managing with the kitchen table, which gets inconvenient at meal times.' He smiled again, his teeth white in his tanned face.

She attached a 'sold' label to the desk, and waved a hand towards the stairs. 'If you'll come down to the office I'll make a note of your address.'

'And take my money,' he said, following her.

'A necessary evil,' she agreed, and turned to him as they reached the shop floor. 'By the way, if your sister doesn't like the mirror we'll exchange it for something else, or refund the money.'

'Lydia will love it,' he said with assurance. 'But if by any chance she doesn't I'll keep it myself.'

And put it in the study with desk? thought Hester, surprised, and showed him into the office. 'I'll just get the mirror packed for you. Would you like it gift-wrapped?'

'I would, indeed. Thank you.'

When Hester returned he accepted a chair, then sat,

watching her, as she recorded details of the mirror's provenance and the pedigree of David's desk.

'I didn't recognise you at first last night,' he said suddenly.

Hester looked up. 'Oh? Why not?'

'It took me some time to realise that the siren in pink with her hair loose was the lady magistrate I'd encountered in the morning.' He eyed her judiciously. 'And today you look different again.'

Hester very deliberately made no response. 'How would you like to pay?' she said crisply.

'By cheque.'

'Of course.' She held out the bill for him, and he bent to write in his chequebook. 'Where shall I send the articles?' she asked, refusing to admit she knew where he lived. 'We deliver anywhere within a thirty-mile radius, but after that we charge so much a mile.'

'Then I'm in luck. I'll write my address on the back.'

'Thank you, Mr Barclay.'

He looked blank for a moment, then smiled a little. 'I suppose we never were formally introduced, Mrs Conway. My name's actually Hazard—Patrick Hazard. The twins are my nephews, and Lydia—their mother—is my sister.'

CHAPTER TWO

'Oн—I beg your pardon.' Taken aback, Hester busied herself with taking down his address. Patrick Hazard, it seemed, lived in the depths of the Gloucestershire countryside in a house called Long Wivutts near the village of Avecote, several miles from Chastlecombe.

'I moved in a couple of days ago,' he explained. 'I'm more or less camping out with the bare necessities, but a desk is my first priority.'

'If you're really urgently in need of it we could get it to you this evening,' offered Hester.

'It seems a bit much on a Saturday evening…' he began, but the idea so obviously appealed to him that Hester shook her head.

'No trouble, Mr Hazard. If someone brings it round about seven—will you be in, then?'

'Yes. My brother-in-law came home this morning, so I'm free to get back to my own place. In confidence, Ms Conway, he flatly refused to let Lydia go to court with the twins in her present condition, so I volunteered for the job and took the boys back to school afterwards.' His face hardened. 'Which is probably a good thing—gives their father time to simmer down before he fetches them home for the summer.'

Hester made no comment. She got up and handed him the detailed provenances. 'Thank you, Mr Hazard. I hope you're happy with the desk.'

'I can hardly fail to be. It's exactly what I had in

mind,' he assured her, rising quickly. He held out his hand. 'Thank you for your help, Mrs Conway.'

'Not at all. Thank you for your custom.' She shook the hand briefly, then preceded him out into the shop. 'Are you taking the mirror now, or shall we deliver it with the desk?'

'Now, please.' He complimented Sheila on her artistic skill, then took the large, beribboned box and with a smile of farewell at Hester went out into the sunlit square, where the bright afternoon light glinted on strands of silver in his thatch of blond hair.

'Very nice,' said Sheila softly, and Hester grinned.

'He spent a nice lot of money, too. Where's Mark?'

'It's his afternoon off, remember? Playing cricket.'

'Oh, *bother*, so he is.'

'Can I do something?' asked Sheila.

'No, thanks. I'll wait until David gets back. If you'll take over for a bit with Iris I'll shut myself up in the office with a sandwich and a cup of coffee.'

Hester often brought a packed lunch on summer Saturdays. Sometimes she went for a walk down to the river and ate it there. At other times, like today, half an hour with a novel was more to her taste. But the encounter with the intriguing Mr Hazard had left her feeling curious, and instead of reading she couldn't help wondering why he needed a desk so urgently—and if there was a Mrs Hazard helping him with the move. Perhaps the need for the desk was due to the lady's sovereignty over her kitchen table.

Hester turned back to her book. Her interest in Patrick Hazard was due solely to the possibility that he might be lacking other furniture that Conway's could provide. Otherwise, whether he had a wife or not was really none of her business.

When David got back Hester asked him if he could possibly deliver a desk out to Avecote that evening. He looked at her in utter dismay.

'Tonight? I've planned an intimate dinner for two, remember? Which I am cooking with my own fair hands. And I rather wanted my evening uninterrupted by thoughts of business, or anything else—other than of bed at the end of it!'

Hester flushed, and gave him an unladylike shove. 'All right, all right, you get on with your cooking and *I'll* deliver the desk.'

'It is one of my efforts, I hope?'

'It certainly is. And I sold that Venetian mirror old Mrs Lawson passed on to us. She'll be thrilled.'

'You *have* been busy. Who bought my desk?'

'A man by the name of Hazard—he bought the mirror, too.'

'Can't Mark deliver them?'

Hester shook her head. 'Cricket match. But don't worry; if you can heave the desk in the car this end, I imagine Mr Hazard can help heave it out at Avecote. He's in a hurry for it, apparently.'

'You're an angel. Thanks, love.' David stooped to kiss her cheek, then went off, whistling, to his workshop, leaving Hester and her attendants with the slowing-off business of Saturday afternoon.

Later, after David and Peter had loaded the muslin-swathed desk into her estate car, Hester drove home and spent some time in the shower. Afterwards, comfortable in old jeans and a white cotton shirt, her newly washed hair gleaming loose on her shoulders, she set off for Avecote, not at all averse to driving through the sunlit summer evening along winding minor roads to avoid the holiday traffic.

Avecote was a typical Cotswold village, nestling in a hollow, with steep-pitched roofs pointing through trees fluttering with the tender green leaves of early summer. She drove slowly along the road which skirted the village, then stopped in a layby a mile or so beyond and consulted a large-scale local map to track down the narrow road Patrick Hazard had mentioned.

Eventually, after careful progress between high hedges along a road with only occasional passing places, she spotted a rutted, unadopted lane which finally led her to the home of Patrick Hazard. Half-hidden at the end of a long drive edged with limes, the familiar Cotswold limestone of the walls glowed like honey in the evening light. The house was typical of the region, with prominent gables, moulded dripcourses round the tops of the window and a beautiful roof of Cotswold stone tiles with the familiar, purpose-built dip to prevent the tiles from shifting.

Long Wivutts was certainly beautiful, but it was also in the middle of nowhere. Hester couldn't help wondering what had attracted Patrick Hazard to such isolation. The garden was wildly overgrown and the house looked strangely somnolent, as though it had been sleeping, undisturbed by tenants, for centuries.

She brought the car to a halt on the gravel in front of the aged oak front door set in an arched stone frame, and almost at once Patrick Hazard emerged, hair wet from a recent shower, his eyebrows raised in astonishment as he saw Hester.

'Mrs Conway! If I'd realised I was putting *you* to such trouble the desk could have waited until Monday—or later.'

Hester shook her head, smiling as she got out. 'It's

only a few miles, and a beautiful evening. It was no trouble at all, other than a bit in finding you. Oddly enough I've never been anywhere near your home patch before, Mr Hazard.'

'My lack of neighbours was the big selling point, other than something which drew me to Long Wivutts the moment I laid eyes on it.'

'I can understand that. It's a beautiful house.' Hester smiled at him apologetically. 'But the main drawback to making the delivery alone is that you're obliged to give me a hand to get the desk inside.'

Patrick Hazard, who was dressed in much the same way as herself, eyed Hester doubtfully. 'Are you sure you can manage that, Mrs Conway? Forgive me for mentioning it, but you're not very big.'

'But well used to heaving furniture around,' she assured him briskly. 'The desk is wrapped in muslin to avoid any knocks, and if we remove the drawers out here it won't be much of a problem—unless your study's in the attic, of course.'

'No, just inside the front door.' He ushered her inside. 'If you take a look, perhaps we can plan a campaign to do the least damage to you or the desk. Or perhaps we could just leave it in the hall and I'll get Wilf Robbins to give me a hand on Monday.' He looked at her face, then said smoothly, 'But that, of course, would cancel your good deed in getting the desk to me tonight.'

The shadowy panelled hall was square, with several wide oak doors opening off it. The first opened into the study, which contained two comfortable chairs flanking a stone fireplace, a couple of small tables, a television, a fax machine and a pile of cardboard boxes.

'Do you want your desk under the window?' asked Hester, sizing up the room.

He sighed. 'Alas, no. If I do I'll keep looking out on the garden and never get down to any work. I thought of putting it on the blank wall over there behind the door.'

'It shouldn't be a problem,' she said briskly. 'These old doors are wide, which is a help. The desk should come in easily enough.'

And, despite Patrick Hazard's doubts about her physical capabilities, fifteen minutes later the beautiful desk was installed, unharmed, against the panelling on the inner wall, with enough space alongside it for one of the tables.

'Which I shall need for my computer,' he said, breathing hard. 'It's a crime to pile a stack of soulless technology on a work of art like your husband's desk.'

Hester, also breathing hard, looked at him sharply. 'This isn't one of my husband's pieces, Mr Hazard. I hope you didn't buy it under that impression. The provenance states very clearly that it's a David Conway original.'

Narrowed green eyes met hers. 'I'm sorry—wires crossed somewhere,' he said, after a pause. 'You're not David Conway's wife?'

'No. I was married to his elder brother.'

'Divorced?'

'No. I'm a widow.'

There was embarrassment, coupled with something less identifiable, in the rueful look he gave her. 'I'm sorry. You were pointed out as the Conways last night—as a couple. I took it for granted you were married. To each other.'

Hester shook her head. 'David's wife has been away visiting her parents this week. Tally's due back about now, which is why David didn't deliver the desk himself. And Mark, who works for us and would have been happy to help normally, is playing cricket. So I volunteered.'

'It's extraordinarily noble of you on a Saturday night.'

'Not at all. I wasn't doing anything.'

'Which is hard to believe,' he said swiftly, then bit his lip. 'I'm sorry. That was probably tactless. How recently were you widowed?'

'Several years ago, Mr Hazard.' She smiled a little. 'And I do have a reasonably busy social life. I just don't happen to have anything planned for tonight.'

'Nothing at all? Then what are you going to do now?'

'Go home and do a bit of gardening, probably. The desk looks happy here. It was a good choice. Goodnight, Mr Hazard.'

He looked at her in silence for a moment, something indefinably different in his manner. 'Now we've established that I'm not the twins' father and you're not David Conway's wife,' he said at last, smiling crookedly, 'would you consider staying for a while to share my supper with me?'

Hester, taken aback for a moment, looked at him thoughtfully. She found that she liked the idea. And there was no reason why she shouldn't accept. She went out with various male friends in Chastlecombe, in the purely platonic way that was all she had to offer. On the other hand, if she said yes to Patrick Hazard—who was, without doubt, the most interest-ing and attractive man she'd met since Richard—it was possible he might misunderstand the situation now he knew she was a widow. Others had before him, taking her attitude as a challenge.

'You're taking such a long time to decide,' he said at last, a wry twist to his mouth, 'I take it the answer's no.'

Hester's curiosity got the better of her. She wanted to know more about this man, why he'd chosen to live here far away from the city lights she felt sure were his usual habitat, what he did for a living. She smiled and shook her head. 'Thank you, I'd like to very much.'

'Wonderful!' The green eyes lit with a dazzling smile. 'Then come this way, Mrs Conway. Let me show you my kitchen—which is the only place to eat, I'm afraid. Or would you like a tour of the house first?'

I would, very much. This is not a house I've ever heard of. I thought I knew most of the interesting places in the Chastlecombe area, but Long Wivutts came as a surprise.'

'The name attracted me before I'd even seen the place.' Patrick led the way across the hall into a sitting room with beautiful panelling, and triple-light latticed windows looking out over the tangled wilderness of the garden. 'I'm told it comes from the size of stone tiles they use on the roofs round here. There are twenty-six sizes, would you believe? All of them with marvellous names like Middle Becks and Short Bachelors. They're pretty difficult to replace now, apparently, though Wilf—the man who's going to help me with the garden—has somehow acquired replacements from some derelict cottage.' He grinned. 'I had the feeling it wouldn't be tactful to enquire about their provenance.'

Hester chuckled. 'Very wise! This is a lovely room—just look at the size of that fireplace. With some chintz-covered sofas and a Persian carpet, maybe, plus a picture or two and some plain, heavy curtains... Sorry. You've probably got it all planned already.'

'Not really. Any suggestions would be welcome.' He led her out into the hall and into a room obviously meant for dining, and then beyond it to a little parlour at the back of the house, both of them as empty as the sitting room. Only the kitchen, which was so large it had obviously been two rooms at one time, was furnished. Late sunlight poured through the windows, washing over a plain round table and four balloon-back Victorian chairs. A bowl of fruit, a basket of eggs and a large bread-crock sat on a counter which ran the length of gleaming oak-fronted cupboards— as new as the cooker and refrigerator, but so severely plain they blended harmoniously with the venerable stone flags underfoot.

'This is perfect,' said Hester with enthusiasm. 'You've caught exactly the right note with the cupboards. Only, in winter I advise a rug or two on this floor—I speak from experience. Mine's the same, and it can be very cold.'

'I must confess the previous owners had got as far as doing up the kitchen and one of the bathrooms,' he admitted. 'I'd like any advice you have to spare. My sister, as must be obvious, isn't at her best at the moment. And when the baby arrives she'll have too much to do to have much time for me. She gave me the table and chairs—too small for Ashdown House.

But she's worried about not giving more of a helping hand here. I told her I'm big enough and old enough to look after myself. She's older than me—still thinks of me as the little brother.'

Hester smiled. It was hard to imagine Patrick Hazard as a kid brother. 'If you do need advice and I can supply it, I'll be happy to. But, for the time being, if you'll show me what you had in mind for a meal I'll put it together—if you like.'

'I just meant you to share the meal, not prepare it for me!' he said swiftly.

'Just tell me what you had in mind and I can make a start.' She smiled mischievously. 'I'm hungry. So if I lend a hand we'll eat all the sooner.'

He bowed in defeat, then opened the refrigerator and took out the ingredients for a very respectable cold meal—salad greens, tomatoes, cheese, half a ham. He looked at her levelly. 'You know, this is very good of you. I had expected to spend a solitary evening.'

So had Hester, who was more charmed by the prospect of dinner with Patrick Hazard than she cared to admit. And the informality of helping with the meal only added to the charm. While she set eggs to boil and washed salad greens her host laid the table, then took a bottle of champagne from the refrigerator.

'I thought we might celebrate my first dinner guest with this,' he announced.

Hester hesitated, then smiled ruefully. 'Mr Hazard, I dislike wine of any kind. Vintage champagne would be utterly wasted on me.'

'Then we'll drink something else,' he said promptly. 'But only if you call me Patrick.'

She nodded, smiling. 'I'm Hester.'

'I know.'

They looked at each other for a moment, then Hester took the pan of eggs from the hob and ran cold water over them at the sink. 'I shall be perfectly happy with a glass of this, straight from the tap,' she said over her shoulder.

'Does your dislike of wine extend to alcohol in general?'

'I enjoy a Pimm's as a rare summer treat, and I keep brandy in the house for emergencies. But wine I really dislike.' She looked up from peeling the eggs. 'When I was a student I was afraid to admit it—bad for the image—so I drank it and suffered the consequences. I'm a bit wiser now.'

'Which must be a generally held opinion locally since you were asked to be a magistrate.' He took a loaf of bread from the crock and began slicing it. 'Though you can't have been on the bench for long.'

'Just over a year now, but I still feel like a beginner. I did all the usual courses, naturally, and I shall go on doing others in the future. For legal instruction I rely on people like John Brigham—he's the barrister who usually acts as clerk of the court.' Hester halved the eggs and took out the yolks. 'Are those handsome cupboards empty, or have you anything I can use to make a dressing and so on?'

Patrick Hazard's store cupboards were surprisingly well-stocked. With hot pepper sauce to devil the eggs, and balsamic vinegar and olive oil to dress the salad, the meal they sat down to a little while later was simple, but very much to Hester's taste. It was completed with a large, ice-filled goblet of bottled Cotswold spring water, which her host produced in preference to the alternative straight from the tap.

'I got some of that in for Lydia,' he said, pouring himself a beer. He raised his glass to her in toast. 'To my unexpected but very welcome guest. I'm only sorry the dinner isn't more in keeping with the occasion.'

Hester shook her head as she helped herself to ham. 'This is exactly my kind of meal. I wouldn't have done nearly as well at home. I tend to get tired by Saturday night. If I'm not going out I usually don't bother too much about dinner.'

Patrick offered the basket of bread. 'Hester, since circumstance has thrown us so unexpectedly together, I own to curiosity. Will you allow me to ask questions?'

She took a slice and buttered it thoughtfully. 'About myself?'

'Yes.' He smiled. 'I'll respond in kind, if you like. Fair?'

'Fair,' she agreed, equally curious to learn about Patrick. 'What would you like to know?'

'Anything you care to tell me. For a start, are you a native of Chastlecombe?'

'No. If it hadn't been for a certain baby I might never have come to the place, other than as a tourist. I got a job at Queens High School as a replacement for the history teacher while she was away on maternity leave.' Hester drank some of her water. 'Richard Conway was on the board of governors. He was in his early forties, and a confirmed bachelor. I was late twenties and, I thought, a career educationist. Wrong on both counts.'

She smiled crookedly. 'We were married the day after the school closed for the summer holidays. And instead of applying for another teaching post I went into the business with Richard. David was still in college then. So I involved myself in the shop and the buying, leaving Richard free to do what he did best—create beautiful furniture.'

Patrick regarded her steadily, then leaned over to refill her glass. 'What happened to him, Hester?'

'He died of a sudden, massive heart attack while we were on holiday in France, celebrating our first anniversary.'

Patrick let out a deep breath. 'Poor young bride,' he said very quietly.

Hester looked away. 'Afterwards Richard's family were very good to me. They persuaded me to stay in the business, so I did.'

Patrick got up and took their plates, then returned with the fruit bowl and pushed the platter of cheese towards her.

Hester accepted a crisp green apple. 'Your turn, then, Patrick. You're a lawyer, of course?'

He nodded. 'Guilty. How did you know?'

'Your bow to the bench was a bit of a giveaway.'

'Reflex action. Though I've retired from actually practising law.'

'Retired?' She eyed him curiously. 'Aren't you a bit young for that?'

'I've taken up another career,' he said blandly. 'But I used to be a city lawyer, working in the London office of a New York-based firm, earning a quite outrageous salary. UK law governs project and corporate deals in Europe and Asia, and global-minded American law firms tend to hire UK lawyers to stay on top of the competition. And as the icing on the cake I shared a flat with the gorgeous Alicia, who earned a six-figure salary in advertising.'

Hester listened in awe. It all sounded a long way from the laid-back lifestyle of Chastlecombe.

'On one of my trips to the Washington office I took Alicia with me and introduced her to an American colleague, Jay Benedict the Third.' He smiled crookedly. 'Big mistake. Jay earned more than I did, and his daddy's rich, too. Jay's also an ex-college quarterback, half a head taller than me—all shoulders and flashing white smile. *And* a brilliant lawyer, the swine.'

Hester let out an involuntary giggle.

Patrick grinned. 'I gave them my blessing through clenched teeth, flew back to London and proceeded to expand the office and make an even bigger packet for myself. Then one day I took a good look at myself and didn't much like what I saw. After some soul-searching I resigned and became a defence lawyer with a firm where I did as much legal aid work as the more remunerative stuff. I trust,' he added, 'that you are now full of respect for my U-turn?'

'Deeply impressed,' agreed Hester. 'So why did you retire?'

'I'm coming to that. Let's have some coffee?'

When they were settled in the study, Patrick went on. 'So now, dear reader, we come to the really interesting bit. After Alicia's desertion I worked twice as hard, but the playing no longer appealed. So in the long winter evenings I began to write a book—a novel about a hot-shot, materialistic lawyer and the various cases, lost and won, that bring him, with help from the woman he loves, to a final, shattering epiphany. The realisation that there's more to life than possessions. Corny, I know. But it worked. It comes out here next month, and it's already been auctioned off in the

States. And there's a pretty good chance of film rights.'

'In that case,' said Hester, with a smile, 'you should soon be able to run to some furniture for this place.'

'From Conway's, of course?' he said swiftly.

Hester coloured to the roots of her hair, angry because she felt so hurt. She looked at her watch and got up. 'It's late. I must go.'

Patrick jumped to his feet and caught her hands. 'I was *joking*, Hester. Please stay.'

She shook her head, feeling suddenly tired. 'I won't, thank you. I'm entertaining a guest for Sunday lunch tomorrow. I'll need an early start.'

Ignoring her attempts to withdraw them, Patrick kept hold of her hands. 'Hester,' he said urgently. 'I never thought for a moment that you were drumming up trade. Damn,' he added bitterly, 'I'm not usually so maladroit.'

She stared down at their clasped hands, unwilling to indulge in a struggle she was unlikely to win. 'Thank you for the meal,' she said at last, and the grasp on her hands relaxed.

'Any thanks involved are due to you, not me,' he said quietly. 'It was very good of you to drive out here with the desk.'

Hester looked up, meeting his frowning green gaze very directly. 'I often make deliveries. Even on Saturday evenings. It's all part of the Conway service. Now, I really must go.

Outside, the wild, tangled garden was bleached free of colour in a twilight scented with warm earth and new-mown grass.

Patrick breathed in deeply. 'I would like to be your friend, Hester.' His voice was crisp and incisive, almost startling in the stillness. 'It seems a shame to let one ill-considered flippancy prevent that. Unless the idea of friendship with me is anathema to you, of course.'

It wasn't in the slightest. And taking umbrage with a potential customer was a touch immature for a thirty-something widowed lady, thought Hester, recovering her sense of humour. She smiled at Patrick with sudden, deliberate warmth.

'It's not. I'm sorry. I was touchy.' And, to prove she had recovered, her smile deepened. 'But I'm not proud. Joking or not, if you do need any furniture you know where to come.'

'I may take you up on that.' His smile was just visible as a show of white in his sun-bronzed face. 'Can't I persuade you to tour the house again, give me advice about what I need?'

'Could we leave that for another day—?' She stopped, flushing.

'Certainly—when?' asked Patrick promptly. 'Not tomorrow, I know. Is your lunch guest male or female?'

'Male,' said Hester, oddly flattered. 'A regular arrangement. We alternate. Sometimes I cook lunch for him, sometimes he takes me out.'

'Would he object if I did this?' He bent suddenly and kissed her surprised mouth. 'Which means I've really scuppered myself now,' he said, stepping back. 'So I may as well go the whole hog and admit that last night I was furious with myself for feeling attracted to another man's wife—one who was playing around with Galbraith all night, to add to my joys.'

'Oh, I see,' she said in sudden comprehension.

'That's why you were eyeing me with such disapproval.'

'I'm surprised you noticed. You kept your distance.'

'I thought the pregnant lady with you was your wife. And I'd been on the bench when her sons were in court. Of course I kept away from you—both of you!'

'Is Galbraith a close friend?' he asked bluntly.

'I wonder what you mean by close?' she said, raising an eyebrow. 'Tim's just a friend. Like all my men-friends, he keeps to the rules.'

'Whose rules?'

'Mine.'

'Tell me what they are and I'll keep to the letter of your law, I promise. Though I admit to a dislike of the sound of "all". Are there that many?'

'Three, if you're counting. One's a widower, another's recovering from a divorce and Tim harbours a much-publicised allergy to marriage.'

Patrick moved closer to peer down into her face. 'If I want to be your friend do you expect me to be one of this crowd of yours?'

'I don't expect anything of you,' she retorted. 'Until yesterday I didn't know you existed.'

He laughed suddenly. 'How true. All right, let's start again. If I stick to your rules like glue will you let me take you out to a proper dinner one night next week?'

She looked at him for a moment, then nodded. 'Yes, thank you. I will.'

'Then come back in and let me make you some more coffee. You can't go home yet. It's early.'

When she eyed him doubtfully Patrick grinned and

held up his right hand. 'I swear to behave like a monk, so come back inside. Please.'

It was late before Hester left to drive home, mainly because Patrick had kept his word and made no more attempts to touch her—while at the same time, in some unspoken way, managing to make it quite clear he would have liked to. It was flattering, and added zest and an underlying element of spice to their conversation. Patrick's kiss had been sudden but not threatening, and while she'd felt no response to it she had a feeling that, if he'd persisted, she might have.

He was a very attractive man. Not handsome in a movie-star way, but his colouring, clever face and clipped, assured voice combined to form a very potent form of charm. Alone among the men she'd known since Richard, he touched a chord inside her. A matter of wavelength rather than physical chemistry. Even on such short acquaintance she felt very much in tune with him. And knew, without being told, that he felt the same towards her.

While they despatched a new pot of coffee Patrick talked about his London flat, loaned, for the time being, to house-hunting friends.

'I had thought of transferring some of the furniture down here until I have time to decide what this house would like, but in the circumstances I had to leave everything there for my temporary tenants and content myself with the bare rudiments in my bucolic retreat,' he said, looking relaxed and, to Hester, physically elegant in a way peculiarly his own—as if every part of him was put together with such precision he could move in any way he chose and never look awkward or ungraceful.

Very different from Richard.

'Do you intend to keep your London flat?' she asked.

'Definitely. I've never lived in the country before. I might find it hard to settle down here.'

'While I'm a real country cousin,' said Hester lightly.

'And happy to stay that way?'

'Yes. I lead a busy, pleasant life here.' She looked towards the desk. 'Are you writing another novel?'

'I certainly am, which is why I need a desk so badly. I keep losing the various books of reference I'm using for research.' Patrick smiled at her. 'I enjoy writing, but I'm not the world's most efficient researcher. I get too absorbed in the text and forget to make notes.'

'Is this another legal story?'

He nodded. 'But a period one this time. Turn of the century. A *cause célèbre*-type case with a beautiful woman accused of murder, and the defending counsel who gets her off.'

'Sounds fascinating.' Hester got up. 'If you can't get up to London for research material the Chastlecombe public library is very well equipped— or they'll find books for you if they aren't in stock.'

'Good idea—I'll join next time I'm in the town.' He walked outside with her into the still, starry darkness, which in this remote spot had no streetlights to lessen its intensity. 'It's very peaceful here. I only hope it isn't too peaceful and gives me writer's block.'

'Is that likely?'

'I hope not.' His smile gleamed white in the light above his venerable front door. 'I've been paid a sizeable advance already.'

Hester held out her hand. 'Then the best of luck. I don't think I could function with that kind of pressure.'

Patrick took her hand and held it lightly in his. 'This has been a very good evening for me, Hester. Thank you. I know you're a busy lady. When can I take you out to dinner?'

'I don't have my diary with me.'

'Then I'll ring you.'

As Hester drove away she experienced the oddest sensation, as though she was doing the wrong thing, that she was meant to stay. And, though she'd said nothing to Patrick, on the tour of the empty rooms of Long Wivutts she'd experienced a strong feeling of homecoming, as though she belonged there. Strange. She wasn't the fanciful type. And she'd never even heard of the place before, let alone set foot inside it. Nor, when she'd asked for directions, had David.

When Hester got home she decided to go straight to bed. Tomorrow she was giving her father-in-law lunch, and though Robert Conway was the least critical of men she always felt on her mettle to provide Richard's father with as delicious a meal as she could contrive. It had been Richard who had taught her how to cook. She had learned so much from him in the cruelly short period of their marriage.

Hester got ready for bed, then looked at the photograph on the bedside table. Richard Conway smiled his crooked smile at her, his heavy black hair unruly on his forehead. He had been a large man in every way, in stature and in temperament. A gentle giant with deep, abiding passions, one of which had been his work. Hester had been the other. Richard had never tired of telling her he'd been waiting for her all his life. The only shadow on their union had been the lack of children, a lack Hester had mourned all the more deeply when she'd been left alone after his death.

Hester turned out the light quickly and lay in the dark. At first, in the weeks after Richard had died, she'd talked to his photograph every night. As some people wrote in diaries, she'd communed with Richard—told him about her day, confided her hopes and fears—just as though he'd been alive and in the bed beside her. Not that they had ever talked much in bed. Richard, from the first, had been a sexually demanding husband, and she had responded gladly, always. And had cried many bitter tears in this same bed after he'd died, missing his physical presence. But, if she were totally honest, there had been more actual conversation with his photograph than with Richard when he'd been alive.

Hester lay staring at the stars through the window, wondering why she'd used her lack of diary as a means of avoiding a definite date for another evening with Patrick Hazard. She always knew exactly how her week was arranged, sometimes for weeks in advance, without reference to a diary or any other reminder. And when Tim Galbraith or John Brigham asked her out she always knew instantly whether the dates they suggested were convenient or not. Yet with Patrick she'd hedged a little, giving herself time to—to what? Plead a previous engagement, or put him off altogether? Hester shrugged, unseen, in the dark. One evening was no big deal. It needn't be repeated. If discouraged gently, Patrick Hazard had too much pride to persist.

Hester was on the point of falling asleep when she

discovered why, exactly, Patrick Hazard was to be tactfully discouraged. Tim Galbraith, Edward Moore and John Brigham, the trio she went out with on a fairly regular basis, were not only nice men and good companions, they had one important thing in common: Richard would have had no objection to any of them. Patrick was different. He posed far more of a threat. Unlike the others, for whom she felt nothing warmer than liking, she was strongly attracted to Patrick Hazard. Even on such short acquaintance. But at this stage the attraction was merely cerebral. Whether it would remain that way if she saw more of him was open to question.

So, one evening with him would have to do. And if he wanted more she would have to think of a convincing reason for her refusal. Patrick Hazard would think she was mad if she cited her dead husband's disapproval.

CHAPTER THREE

ROBERT CONWAY rose from the table with a smile of appreciation. 'Excellent lunch, my dear, as always.'

Hester smiled, pleased, as she took their plates. 'Tea?'

'Please, Hester.' His eyes twinkled. 'Not even an indulgent father-in-law like me can praise your coffee.'

'The caffeine's bad for you anyway,' she said, chuckling. 'Would you like it out in the garden? The sun's moved away a bit now.'

When they were settled in deck chairs, Hester in full sun and Robert in the shade of a pear tree, she filled their cups then sat back to enjoy the warm afternoon.

'So what did you do last night?' asked Robert.

'I went out to Avecote to deliver a desk.' Hester looked at his spare, relaxed frame consideringly, then gave him an account of Patrick Hazard, his novel, and his semi-unfurnished home, and included the meal she'd stayed to share, stressing the fact that her motive had been more in the nature of future furniture orders than to eat dinner with Patrick Hazard.

'It sounds like a very interesting evening,' said Robert neutrally. 'Are you seeing him again?'

Hester nodded, feeling irrationally guilty. 'Just once, anyway.'

'Why just once?' said Robert, and fixed her with a probing eye. 'Is he married?'

'No.'

'Yet you say he's interesting, and both clever and attractive. Is he gay?'

'No, nothing like that.'

'Then enjoy his company.' Robert drank his tea tranquilly. 'You've done wonders in this garden, Hester. The blossoms on that cistus are like a fall of snowflakes. Your hydrangeas look healthy, too.'

'They should be, with all the tender loving care I lavish on them.'

'Forgive me for being an interfering old man, but couldn't you find something else to lavish it on?' He smiled to take the sting out of his words. 'You're a handsome young woman, Hester. You should be bringing up a family.'

She winced, and he apologised quickly.

'But these things have to be said. I know your mother is of the same opinion. She would like some grandchildren. So would I.'

'David and Tally will provide you with those,' said Hester.

'You mean that yours wouldn't really be my grand-children?' asked Robert gently, and she shook her head vehemently.

'I didn't mean that at all, Robert. It's just that there's no likelihood of my having a family.'

'Why not? It's years since Richard died. And while neither of us will ever forget him, it's time you found someone else to share your life.'

'No one could replace Richard,' she said huskily.

'I agree. But that isn't what's at issue here. I think it's time you cast off those widow's weeds—'

'I've never worn mourning!' she protested.

'Not on the outside, no,' he agreed. 'Richard,' he

added with gentle emphasis, 'would like you to be happy.'

'I am!'

'Are you?' He smiled wryly. 'You've done all the sensible things, Hester—sold the house you shared with Richard, bought this cottage. You fill your life with the shop, and meetings and lectures and the social life of Chastlecombe, not to mention your work as a magistrate. You've behaved admirably.' His eyes twinkled. 'But at your age you ought to be behaving badly sometimes too. Have some fun, Hester. Richard's dead, but you still have a life to live. And here endeth the lesson. Forgive me for prosing on.'

Hester received his little lecture without protest, mainly because it was the same one her mother delivered every time they were together.

'I do have fun. Sometimes.'

'And by the sound of it your Saturday evening with this man Hazard was one of the times. Add him to your roster of escorts.'

Hester giggled. 'You make it sound like a male harem!'

Patrick Hazard soon made it plain that he was of the same mind as Robert Conway. He rang Hester early next morning, before she left for the shop, asked her if she now had her diary to hand and which nights she had free.

Hester's eyes narrowed at his use of the plural. 'How about Saturday?' she said, after a pause intended to convey perusal of her calendar.

'Not before then?'

'Afraid not. But don't worry,' she added casually.

'If Saturday isn't convenient leave it for another time.'

'Certainly not. Saturday it is. Where would you like to go?'

As far away as possible, Hester thought. The idea of dining with Patrick in one of the haunts popular with Chastlecombe café society held very little appeal. 'Somewhere different,' she said vaguely.

'I'm a stranger in town,' he reminded her. 'As yet I don't know what exactly *is* different for you. I take it you mean somewhere unfrequented by your other— friends.'

'I really don't mind,' she said hastily. 'You choose.'

'Right. I'll work on it and come for you at seven. Where do you live?'

Hester gave him her address, then went off to the shop, feeling she'd done something rash. The feeling grew stronger when Annie Raymond, wife of one of her colleagues on the bench and fellow-member of the history society, rang mid-morning to ask her to dinner the following Saturday.

'I've asked Tim already,' her friend said. 'I thought we'd have a cold supper on the terrace if the weather holds.'

'I'm terribly sorry, Annie,' said Hester, feeling irrationally guilty. 'I'm already doing something on Saturday.'

'Really? Well it can't be with John Brigham, because I've invited him along, too. Going out with Edward, I suppose?'

Hester pulled a face. 'Actually, no.'

There was a silence while Annie waited expect-

antly. When no details were forthcoming, she chuckled.

'In other words, mind your own business, Annie.
Sorry you can't come, Hester, but have fun whatever
you're doing.'

Afterwards Hester cursed herself for being so se-
cretive. She should have said straight away that she
was spending the evening with Patrick Hazard, who
was a relative of the new owners of Ashdown House.
Now she'd made a great mystery of it, and Annie
Raymond would attach far more importance to the
evening than it merited.

'You look fierce,' said David, coming through the
back entrance of the shop. 'Is something wrong?'

'Not exactly. I've just been a bit silly, that's all.'

'Hard to believe, oh sensible one. Do I smell coffee?'

Hester spent her break in the office with David,
asking after Tally's family.

'Her mother's better now, praise be.' He grinned.
'It's very nice to have my lonely bed filled again—'
He broke off, biting his lip. 'Which is a crass lack of
tact on my part, Hester. Sorry.'

She patted his hand. 'It's been a long time now,
David. I'm used to it.'

'Well, you shouldn't be,' he said gruffly. 'High
time you had a husband, or a lover, or whatever takes
your fancy.'

'Have you been talking to your father?' she asked
sharply.

'No. Has he been holding forth on the same theme?
Good for him. Anyway,' he added hastily, at the look
in her eye, 'Tally wants to know which days you're

in court this week. She'll come and help out while you're off.'

'Wonderful.' Hester yawned. 'Just Friday. It would be nice not to come into the shop at all that day, as I doubt I'll get off lightly in court like last week. Thank Tally for me; tell her I owe her one.'

'You don't owe her anything,' said David firmly. 'You do too much—workwise, anyway. Time you played a bit more—' He flung up his hands. 'All right, all right, I'm going.'

The week went by at its usual summer pace, with busy days at the shop and a very protracted day in court, but it was different in one significant way—Hester was nervous about the forthcoming evening with Patrick Hazard. Several times she tried to think up convincing excuses to back out, but it was difficult to plead illness when she was on public view six days a week in obvious rude health. She thought of pleading a sudden need to visit her mother, but that lady was away on a visit herself, to friends in Dorset. Not that Patrick would know that, but Hester baulked at too elaborate a lie.

And in the end she did nothing, and spent her evenings watering her garden and composing a talk she was giving to the history society the following week. For once she had no other engagements, and by the time Saturday came Hester had forgotten her qualms. After five evenings of her own undiluted company she would probably, she thought irritably, have welcomed an evening with Jack the Ripper.

Hester had rather expected to hear from Patrick again beforehand, but when she returned to the cottage at six o'clock on the Saturday the only message was from Annie, commanding Hester to dinner the following Saturday instead, since half her guests of this week were down with summer flu. Edward Moore had rung Hester at the shop about a concert in the Assembly Rooms the following week. But she'd heard nothing from Patrick.

The evening was hot and sunny, and at six-forty-five Hester was ready in a black sleeveless dress likely to suit whatever venue Patrick chose for their evening. When the doorbell rang promptly at seven she made herself stay where she was for a count of three before going to open the door—then stood, surprised, at the sight of a smiling, sunburned Patrick, attired in well-worn jeans and open-necked cricket shirt, with battered old desert boots on his feet.

'Good evening, Hester—damn, I meant to ring to suggest casual gear.' He smiled wryly. 'You look stunning, but a tad elegant for the evening I've planned...'

'Then I'll change,' she said promptly, and waved him to a chair. 'Please sit down. Would you like a drink?'

'No thanks; I'm driving, remember.'

But how far, and where exactly? was the burning question. Upstairs in her room, Hester decided to take him at his word. Minutes later she ran downstairs in jeans bleached colourless with age, a navy sleeveless T-shirt and a bright pink cotton shirt worn open with the sleeves rolled up. On her feet she wore grubby striped espadrilles, and, in place of the former *soignée* twist, a blue ribbon scrunchie gathered her hair into a ponytail.

'Much better,' Patrick approved, jumping up. 'Right then, Hester. Let's go.'

She switched on lights and drew curtains, then locked up behind her as they left the cottage. 'Where, exactly, are we going?'

'Wait and see,' he said teasingly. 'But I'll give you a clue. It's a riverside location.'

Hester went through the gate he held open for her, rather surprised to see that instead of the Aston Martin or XJS she'd have expected a successful city lawyer to drive Patrick's choice of transport was a workman-like Jeep.

He tossed her up into the passenger seat without ceremony, then leapt in and drove off. Instead of turning left into the town centre, to Hester's relief he took a minor road that led to open country.

'Where *are* we going?' she asked, unable to contain her curiosity. 'Somewhere very informal, I hope.'

'Very.' Patrick grinned, keeping his eyes on the road ahead. 'It's a surprise. In the meantime, tell me about your week. Have you been busy?'

'Non-stop,' she assured him, glad he had no idea exactly how much her evenings had dragged. 'How about you?'

'I've got my study in shape now, so I managed to get some work done. Otherwise I've made very little progress with the house. Wilf Robbins—I believe I mentioned him?—has a wife who will come in and tidy me up a couple of times a week, once I acquire something to tidy. But,' he added with relish, 'in the meantime she will provide me with dinner every other night.'

'You're lucky,' said Hester, impressed. 'It's not easy to find domestic help in these parts. Is Mrs Robbins expensive?'

'No idea. She stated her price and I'm paying it.

Gladly. She's a great cook. Hang on; we turn off here, and the road's a bit rough.'

Patrick was right. For a couple of miles they bumped along a narrow road in need of resurfacing, and, just when Hester felt her rear end was in danger of permanent bruising, Patrick turned the car down a cart track lined with hedges in full summer leaf. Half a mile further on Patrick manoeuvred the vehicle into a space alongside a farm gate.

'From here we walk,' he announced, and got out to lift Hester down. He reached over into the back and removed a rug, which he handed his mystified companion with a ceremonious bow. Then he heaved a large picnic basket out, locked the car and beckoned her down a turning so narrow that Hester hadn't noticed it was there. More like a green tunnel than a path, it led, dry and slippery with dust, through trees which met overhead. After a while it dipped sharply, tree-roots providing shallow steps in the path as they descended towards the sound of running water.

'Here we are,' said Patrick as they arrived at the stream. They walked along the path for a while until they came to a wider part of the bank, complete with willows. 'Spread the rug, Hester, and I'll lay dinner. Do sit down.'

Hester chuckled as she subsided on the rug. 'I was worried you were taking me somewhere grand— hence the black dress.'

Patrick shot her a searching glance then opened the basket and took out mineral water and beer, and put the bottles in the shallows to keep cool. 'I thought the black dress was to remind me you're still in mourning.'

Hester sobered abruptly. Was he right? Had that

been her real motive? 'I thought it would do for whatever type of place you were taking me—I hadn't bargained on a picnic.'

'I didn't mention it in case the weather turned sour on me.' He laid a small tablecloth on the grass with a flourish and took cutlery, plates and napkins from the basket, laying two places with precision. 'Courtesy of Mrs Wilf, I can offer you chicken and ham pie, home-baked bread rolls, sandwiches filled with local salmon in the cook's special lemon mayonnaise, fruitcake and walnut biscuits. I provided the apples, cheese and some tomatoes grown, according to the label, for their flavour—what else would they be grown for, do you think?'

'Colour? Size?' Hester stared in awe at the feast laid out before her. 'No wonder you didn't quibble about wages. Mrs Wilf is obviously worth her weight in gold.'

Patrick served them both with slices of pie, buttered a roll and cut a slice of cheese for Hester, handed her a tomato, then began on his own meal.

'This pie,' she said indistinctly, 'is glorious.'

'You should have tasted the rabbit stew she provided me with the other night!' Patrick rolled his eyes heavenwards. 'Yet Wilf is like a beanpole. A mystery, since his wife assures me he eats second helpings every night, plus a pudding. She was quite upset when she found I had rabbit stew left over for lunch— thought I hadn't enjoyed it since it didn't disappear in one go.'

'Local rabbit, no doubt.'

'Very local. They're all over the place at Long Wivutts. And this salmon, I fear, was poached in more ways than one!'

It was very peaceful beside the stream, where the trickling water was the only sound to break the stillness other than the distant lowing of cows herded home for milking.

'All this is a far cry from your former existence,' said Hester, moving on to a sandwich. 'Or is this research for your novel?'

He nodded. 'There's something very seductive about a meal eaten alfresco—with the company of one's choice,' he added, meeting her eyes.

She received the look without turning away. 'Thank you for the compliment.'

'How old did you say you were, Hester?'

'Thirty-four.'

'Amazing. You look so young in that get-up. Was yours a passionate marriage?' he added, taking her breath away.

For a moment she wanted to flare at him and tell him to keep off something so very beautiful and private. But there was no prurient curiosity in the steady green gaze, only sympathy—and something else which Hester narrowed down to a certain pleasure he was taking in just looking at her. The sunset light was glowing red-gold through the leaves of the sheltering tree, striking fiery sparks from his hair—and probably from her own.

'Yes,' she said simply. 'It was. Could I have some water, please?'

Patrick got up to fill their glasses from the bottles cooling in the stream. He set them beside their plates, then let himself down again on the rug beside her, all his movements economical and graceful. How different from Richard. Her husband, large and sometimes unaware of his own size, had often knocked things over, despite his delicacy with a chisel. But when he'd made love to her he'd been gentleness personified. To start with, at least.

'You're blushing. What are you thinking about?' Patrick demanded.

'It's the sunset light. You look as though you're blushing, too,' she said, not altogether truthfully.

Patrick raised a quizzical eyebrow, then turned the conversation to his sister and the forthcoming arrival, who was due to put in an appearance the following month. 'Jack's worried, and doing his best not to let Lydia know. Which is a laugh; she knows what he's thinking before he does.' He reached over to the basket and cut another slice of pie, offering it to her. Hester shook her head, and he put it on his own plate. 'Lydia's had a couple of miscarriages over the years, and I gather they'd given up the idea of any more babies. This one was a bit of a shock to them both. The afterthought, as Lydia refers to her. But she's thrilled. Because of her age she had an amniocentesis and knows it's going to be a girl.'

They discussed the forthcoming event amicably, Hester interested in the twins' reaction to a sister eighteen years younger than themselves.

'They were hideously embarrassed at first. One's parents don't do that kind of thing, you know,' said Patrick, poker-faced.

'Absolutely not,' agreed Hester, chuckling. 'Are they more reconciled to it now?'

'Lydia's been pretty unwell all the way through, so they're very anxious about her. Now all they want is for the baby to arrive safely and their mother to be all right.'

'Amen to that,' said Hester soberly. 'No wonder you took her place in court.'

'Only after heated argument.' Patrick grimaced. 'She's pretty fierce when it comes to her cubs.'

'I can sympathise with that. I think I would be—' She broke off, turning away to look at the reflected sunset light in the water.

'You have no children. Mrs Cowper told me,' he added as she stiffened. 'Would you have liked a family?'

She turned to look at him, her smile crooked. 'It's not a subject I normally discuss, but, yes, both of us wanted children.'

'You miss him still,' he said softly.

She nodded dumbly.

'Is that why you've never remarried?'

'It's one of the reasons.'

'What are the others?'

'No one's ever asked me, for one thing!' She gave him a belligerent look. 'How about you?'

'No one's ever asked me, either,' he said with mock pathos.

'How about what's-her-name, the one who dumped you for a wealthier prospect?'

'Alicia.' Patrick lay near her feet, his chin propped on an elbow. 'We preferred things the way they were. Just as well. It made everything a lot less complicated when she met Jay Benedict.'

'If you'd been married maybe she wouldn't have—'

'Oh, yes, she would. I was witness to their first meeting. Two clever, street-wise adults suddenly knocked for six the moment they set eyes on each other.' The corners of his mouth went down. 'It's bad for the male ego to watch one's woman fall in love with some other guy at first sight.'

'Were you very hurt?'

He shrugged. 'My pride took a bashing, but I can't pretend I was heartbroken. Having seen it happen at first hand, I realised that I had never really been in love with Alicia myself. We got on well together, in bed and out of it. She's a sexy lady, and very good-looking, great company and a good friend. I missed her—but not for long.' Patrick shrugged. 'I don't think I'm capable of the all-consuming love that blots everything else out. I prefer good companionship and rapport—mental as well as physical. I can't imagine going off my food for a woman, or wanting to kill myself because the object of my affections preferred another bloke.'

'What a pity,' said Hester lightly. 'You're missing out. And who knows? The great passion may happen to you one day, whether you want it or not.'

'I assume that's how you felt about your husband?'

'I was in love with him, yes.' She got to her knees to pack the picnic basket, but Patrick rolled over and caught her by the wrist.

'Do you still feel like that about him?'

Hester looked at the slim, strong fingers holding her captive. 'I still love Richard, if that's what you're asking.'

Patrick released her and sprang to his feet with the graceful economy Hester already found so familiar. 'He was a lucky man.'

'Not so very lucky. He died young,' she said flatly, folding the cloth. 'Would you pass me the napkins, please?'

Patrick handed them over, and retrieved an errant

fork from the grass. 'I meant he was lucky to have a wife who would stay in love with him so long after his death.'

Hester had never discussed her relationship with Richard at all, not even with her mother. And she felt astonished that she was able to do so now, with a man she hardly knew. Everyone else, other than Robert Conway, avoided the subject like the plague.

'You don't understand,' she said matter-of-factly. 'It's obvious that you've never actually been in love. After all this time I don't have the same feelings for him that I had when he was alive, because...'' She hesitated. 'I suppose I mean that, without being able to *make* love, my feeling for him is a more cerebral thing.'

Patrick nodded, his concentration on her explanation absolute, as though he were weighing up evidence brought before him in court. 'Do you still live in the same house?' he asked after a pause.

'No. We had a place a few miles outside Chastlecombe. We drove in together every day. But the house and the garden were too big for me on my own, so I sold it when Richard died and bought the cottage where you picked me up earlier.' She smiled ruefully. 'Believe me, I've done all the right things, Patrick. Moved house, kept up my old interests, even agreed to sit on the bench. I haven't wallowed in my widowhood.'

'Yet you still grieve,' he said without emphasis, closing the basket.

Hester busied herself with shaking grass from the rug before folding it, thinking carefully before she answered. 'No,' she said slowly. 'I don't. Time does mend things, though at first I couldn't imagine that. I still miss Richard, but I don't grieve any more.'

'Good,' said Patrick briskly, and hefted the basket. 'We'd better get back to the car before the light fades. This path is a bit tricky.'

Hester was deep in thought as they walked back, glad that keeping to single file in places ruled out any conversation until they were in the car. This evening, she reminded herself, had been intended as a one-off. But now that she was in Patrick's company—and enjoying it—she couldn't see quite why she'd decided that. Richard wouldn't have disapproved of a man who just wanted to be friends—a man who had no intention of losing his heart to any woman, herself included.

'We're much nearer my place than yours,' said Patrick once they'd reached a main road. 'Will you come home with me and watch television, or listen to music, or just talk for a while?'

It was still very early by Saturday-night-out standards. Hester neither pleaded fatigue nor wanted to. 'Yes, thank you. I'd like that.'

'Thank the Lord for that,' said Patrick piously, glancing at her. 'Does it always take you so long to say yes?'

'It depends on the request!'

He laughed, and reached out a hand to touch hers fleetingly. 'And from now on I promise to ask no more personal questions. 'Not,' he added, with a glittering sideways glance, 'that I mind if you want to ask *me* any.'

When they arrived at Long Wivutts Patrick unlocked the front door and waved Hester in—and immediately the same, strong feeling swept over her, the odd, undeniable feeling of belonging. The first time, then, had not been imagination.

'What is it?' said Patrick, in tune at once to her mood.

'You'll laugh,' said Hester tersely.

'Not if you don't want me to.'

She gave him a faint, uneasy smile. 'I just feel as though I've been here before—and not just last week.'

Patrick gave her a narrowed, searching look, then led the way to the kitchen. 'Would you believe that I feel the same? When I decided to get a weekend place somewhere Jack Barclay told me there was a house going for a song not too far from them. Frankly, I wasn't keen on somewhere so isolated. But my editor wants this book by the end of the summer, and in London I just couldn't seem to get on. So to please Lydia I came to look at the house. And the moment I set foot in it I felt as though I'd lived here all my life.' He dumped the picnic basket on the table and eyed her questioningly. 'And you actually feel something similar?'

Hester nodded, and opened the basket to take out the used plates. 'It's not unusual. When I was house-hunting with Richard there were some I knew I couldn't live in the minute the door was opened to let us in. Whereas in others I felt comfortable straight away.' She put the plates in the sink and turned on the hot tap, remembering that Richard hadn't shared her reactions, and had laughed at her indulgently.

She shot a look at Patrick. 'I wasn't going to tell you this; it seemed so bizarre. When I first arrived I didn't notice anything because we were so occupied with getting the desk in. But when you showed me round I experienced an intense feeling of familiarity—

and welcome. And when I drove away that night it felt all wrong to be leaving. As though something—someone—wanted me to stay.' She shook her head. 'Sounds far-fetched, I suppose.'

'Not to me,' said Patrick emphatically. He began to put the remains of their picnic away in the refrigerator, deep in thought. He turned to look at her. 'The house isn't haunted, Hester. I'm sure of that.'

She nodded. 'So am I.' She smiled suddenly. 'Of course, I haven't been upstairs. Maybe you've got a mad wife in the attic.'

'Ah—a Brontë fan,' he said dryly. 'Right, come on. Leave those. We'll go on a tour.'

A carved bannister edged the polished oak stairs which led, by way of two sharp right turns, to the upper floor. On the broad landing Patrick showed her into the main bedroom. It held a large bed, a carved wooden chair, some luggage and an armoire which dated, Hester felt sure, from the time the house had been built.

'I picked that up in a sale in Hereford last week,' he said. 'Like it?'

'Very much.'

'I thought you might be offended that I hadn't come to you.'

'We don't deal in antique furniture,' she reminded him. 'Nor, I hope, am I that petty. Besides, it looks perfectly at home here.'

'I decided on antique pieces for my own room, but there are three others. I'll convert the one next door into a second bathroom and link it in some way to this one with the help of a sympathetic craftsman, if I can find one. Long Wivutts was built long before the advent of *en suite* plumbing.'

'I can help you there,' said Hester. 'Or David can. He knows everyone skilled in the area.'

'Good. I'll take you up on that. In the meantime the only bathroom is along here. As I told you before, the couple I bought the place from modernised it, but, praise be, their taste didn't run to whirlpool baths and so on.'

The bathroom was very restrained. Plain white porcelain fittings and heavy brass taps, more oak cupboards and a crimson carpet on the floor were very much to Hester's taste.

The other bedrooms were empty, except for the fireplaces that were a feature in every room in the house. And the same feeling of familiarity.

'Are you up to a trip to the attic to make sure it's unoccupied?' said Patrick.

Hester nodded enthusiastically. 'Since we're both dressed for it, why not? Perhaps there's something valuable up there that's been overlooked.'

'I wish!'

The stairs to the attic were hidden in what Hester had assumed was an airing cupboard. The steps were steep and narrow and Patrick went before her, opening a door at the top. He reached inside and switched on a light, then ducked his head and went through the low doorway. Hester followed him and stepped into a long, dimly lit roofspace to find Patrick in the middle of the bare-board floor.

He smiled. 'Due to the steep angle of the roof this is the only place I can stand upright.'

Hester, several inches shorter, had no such problem. The smell of dust and old wood was strong, and it was hot and stuffy in the enclosed space after the long hours of June sunlight. But it was empty. 'No Mrs Rochester, then.'

'Nor any forgotten old masters,' he agreed. 'It was like this when I came. Swept bare. I had rather hoped there might be some old records or papers of some kind to give me an idea about the history of Long Wivutts. But there was nothing. According to the estate agent, it was like this when he went over the place to put it up for sale.'

Hester took a long look round, then shrugged. 'Nothing here at all.'

'No,' agreed Patrick, and stooped to join her. 'No Mrs Rochester, no ghosts, and not much air, either. Let's go down.'

Back in the kitchen Patrick made coffee, put the fruitcake from their picnic on the tray and made for the study, which looked much the same as the previous week, except that the new desk was totally covered by books held open with paperweights.

'My research.' He set the tray down on the table. 'Will you pour, Hester?'

They had demolished half the cake between them and drunk the coffeepot dry before Patrick leaned back in his chair and gave Hester a rather wry smile.

'I fully intended taking you out for the most elegant, expensive dinner I could, probably with the idea of impressing you. Then it occurred to me that wherever we went locally, unless we drove miles outside the area, we would probably meet someone you know.'

'Would that have mattered?' she said, surprised.

'Not to me. How about you?'

'It might have,' she admitted.

'We would certainly not have touched on the subjects we discussed on our picnic.' Patrick smiled. 'Which was the object of the exercise. It occurred to me that I would never get to know you well if we restricted our meetings to public places where Hester Conway is a well-known figure.'

She smiled. 'That's true. And while we're being so honest with each other I may as well admit I intended tonight to be a one-off, whether you wanted to see me again or not.'

CHAPTER FOUR

His eyes narrowed, and he leaned forward slightly in his chair. 'Did you, now? Have you changed your mind?'

'Yes.'

Patrick leaned back again, his eyes quizzical. 'Why?'

'Why the one-off, or why did I change my mind?'

'Both.'

Hester shrugged. 'After I accepted your invitation I got cold feet, but I couldn't bring myself to cancel.'

'Why not?'

'I couldn't think of a good reason. Indisposition was out; I'm on display every day.'

'Why did you regret saying yes? You go out with other men. And,' he added, with a twist to his mouth, 'you didn't appear to take a really strong dislike to me, as far as I could tell.'

'True. But Richard knew the other men, and wouldn't have minded. I had a feeling he might object to you.'

'Why?'

'Because I feel a certain rapport with you that I don't with the others,' she said bluntly, burning her boats. 'If he were alive Richard would be jealous of you.'

He stared at her incredulously. 'After all this time do you still organise your life with an eye to your dead husband's approval?'

'Yes,' said Hester simply. 'I do.'

'So what changed your mind about telling me to get lost after tonight?'

'I had no way of knowing whether you'd want to see me any more,' she said, flushing, 'but—'

'Don't lie. You knew damn well I'd want to see you again,' he said flatly.

'But if you did,' she went on doggedly, 'I felt it would be all right. Once you made your position plain.'

Patrick frowned. 'What position?'

'That you prefer a woman as a friend. Richard wouldn't object to that.'

'Richard,' he said with sudden ferocity, 'can't object to anything, Hester. Painful though it is for you, he's dead. And you're alive. None of us knows what's round the corner, thank God. But next week—tomorrow—you or I could be run over by a car, or struck by lightning. Let's hope we're not. But in the meantime, before death or old age overtake us, surely it's only human to want to live what life we're allocated to the full?'

Hester shrank back in her seat before his intensity, and Patrick, seeing her recoil, calmed down.

'I suppose you've changed your mind again after that outburst?'

She breathed in deeply. 'No. It's not the type of thing I hear on my usual evenings out, but I know you're right. In essence it's much the same thing my father-in-law was saying over Sunday lunch last week—'

'Your father-in-law was your lunch guest?' Patrick interrupted, and smiled suddenly. 'You misled me about him on purpose.'

She shrugged. 'Did I?'

'You know you did.'

They regarded each other in silence for a while, then Patrick gave her a smile which raised the hairs on the back of her neck.

'Time,' he said very softly, 'to put my cards on the table. I do want you for a friend, very much. But I also find you so physically attractive I am exerting great self-control to remain where I am in this chair. Every hormone I possess is clamouring to pull you out of yours and into my arms.'

Hester met his eyes squarely, hoping he couldn't tell that her heart was beating a tattoo against her ribs. 'I did wonder earlier, when you handed me the rug, if you expected me to make love with you on it after the picnic.'

To her surprise Patrick broke into delighted laughter. 'Wanted—not expected! But I do so like a lady who calls a spade a spade.'

Hester grinned, relieved that the sudden sexual tension between them had lessened. 'It avoids misunderstandings.'

Having cleared the air, Hester changed the subject. 'Tonight I was asked to dinner with a friend—'

'One of your entourage?'

'No,' she retorted, unmoved. 'Annie Raymond is a fellow member of the history society, and her husband, Dan, sits on the bench with me sometimes. He's an estate agent.'

'I've met him. He sold me Long Wivutts.' Patrick eyed her challengingly. 'Did you tell Mrs Raymond *why* you were unavailable?'

Hester pulled a face. 'No, I didn't. Which was stupid because she'll ask me, never fear. And because I didn't tell her about you she'll attach too much importance to the whole thing.'

'What thing?' he asked blandly.

'You know very well,' she said irritably.

He grinned. 'But wouldn't the lady have assumed you were socialising with one of your regular trio?'

She shook her head. 'Two of them were invited to dinner, and I admitted I wasn't going out with the third. And in the end Annie postponed the evening, due to the flu bug that's going round.'

Patrick subjected her to a dissecting gaze. 'In future wouldn't it be simpler just to say you're spending time with me? When you agree to, of course,' he added. 'Are you going to do that?'

'Tell her?'

'No. I meant are you going to spend time with me in future?'

Hester was silent for a moment. 'I enjoyed the picnic tonight,' she said elliptically.

'I'll take that as a yes! More coffee?'

Hester accepted, secretly as reluctant to end the evening as Patrick was openly keen to prolong it. She listened, absorbed, when he discussed his novel. He described the growing rapport between the fictional defending counsel and the woman he believes is guilty, even while persuading a jury that she's innocent.

'Does that often happen?' she asked.

'In my profession? Of course it does. The last thing any defending counsel wants is a confession of guilt from his client.'

Patrick changed the subject to tell her how he'd discovered the site for their picnic through his habit of walking in the long summer evenings as a means of relaxing after a day spent in front of a computer screen. 'Wilf knows every blade of grass in this part of the world. He gives me directions, marks down rights of way and footpaths on a diagram, and I set off every night on a sort of mystery tour. Which is how I found our little Eden by the stream. And while I walk I write the next instalment of my book in my head.' He laughed. 'Then I come home and demolish whatever Mrs Wilf has left me, or cook a very unhealthy fry-up.'

It was almost midnight when Patrick stopped the Jeep at Hester's gate. 'There you are, Cinderella—home safe and sound.'

She smiled at him and undid her seat belt. 'Thank you. The picnic was a brilliant idea. My compliments to Mrs Wilf.'

Patrick got out and went round to lift her down. 'I'm glad you enjoyed the evening. I did—enormously.'

To Hester's surprise he released her at once, and made no move to kiss her goodnight, even on the cheek. 'Goodnight, Patrick.'

'Goodnight, Hester. Sleep well.'

Once she was inside her front door he drove off, leaving her with an irritating sense of anti-climax. Which was *really* silly, she fumed, and marched straight upstairs to get ready for bed.

She was lying in the dark, her mind on the odd feeling of belonging she felt at Long Wivutts, when she shot upright in sudden remorse and turned on the light.

'Sorry,' she said to Richard's photograph. 'I forgot to say goodnight.' She smiled guiltily, blew a kiss, then turned out the light and slid down again in the bed. Her mouth drooped in the darkness. Robert was right. So was Patrick. Her much-loved Richard was dead and she was alive. It was time to get on with her life without him.

Hester's phone rang early next morning. 'Hello,' she said, yawning, then woke up sharply to a familiar chuckle in her ear.

'Good morning. I've obviously woken you up.'

Hester looked at the clock. Eight-thirty. 'This,' she said pointedly, 'is the only day of the week I can stay in bed for a while.'

'Sorry,' said Patrick. 'It just occurred to me that we made no mention of another meeting.'

It had occurred to Hester long before they'd parted the night before. 'Didn't we?' she said, yawning again.

'I trust I'm not boring you!'

'Sorry.'

'I forgot to ask if you're entertaining someone to lunch today.'

'No. Someone else is entertaining me.'

'Ah. Then there's no point in my suggesting a drive to some picturesque hostelry for a Sunday roast.'

'Afraid not,' she said, with a sharp pang of regret.

'Pity. Some other time, then.'

'Yes. I'd like that.' When? she thought, waiting expectantly.

'I'll be in touch. Bye, Hester.'

'Goodbye.' She replaced the phone, irritated by her disappointment. Why couldn't Patrick's suggestion have come some other Sunday, when she wasn't doing anything? And, failing that, why couldn't he have fixed a definite time for another meeting?

Hester bit her lip. Only yesterday she had fully intended telling Patrick Hazard she couldn't see him again. She was behaving like a teenager. Less sensibly, if anything, than some of the mature girls she'd encountered during her brief reign as a history teacher.

'Goodness, Hester, you look very brown and glowing today,' said Natalie Conway a few hours later.

'Gardening?' said David, carving roast lamb.

'All morning. Rain is forecast for later, so I had some plants to get in. Then I mowed the lawn, trimmed the edges and did some weeding.' Hester grinned. 'So be warned, I'm hungry!'

Robert Conway examined her unobtrusively as she passed him his plate. 'And what did you do with yourself last night, my dear?'

'I went on a picnic with Patrick Hazard,' said Hester baldly, and helped herself to mint sauce, well-aware of the general astonishment.

'The chap who bought one of my desks?' said David, eyes narrowed. 'Oh, of course—you delivered it to him yourself.'

Hester nodded. 'You were occupied with welcoming Tally back home, if you remember.' She grinned as her young sister-in-law blushed. 'I hope the evening went to plan?'

David nodded smugly. 'It certainly did.'

'Who is this man?' asked Tally eagerly. 'Someone new?'

Aware that Robert was smiling at her in amused approval, Hester described Long Wivutts. She told them that Patrick Hazard was related to the new people at Ashdown House, and was by profession a lawyer who'd taken to writing bestsellers. But she made no mention of the first encounter in court.

'Wow,' said Tally, impressed. 'Sounds interesting. Is his house nice?'

As Hester had known it would, the subject kept the others engrossed for some time. And in some odd sort of way she'd thrown down the gauntlet by admitting she'd gone out with someone other than Tim Galbraith and company. She would feel jolly silly if Patrick didn't ask her out again, because in some way she'd made a declaration of intent. David and Tally didn't realise this, but Robert did—and obviously approved.

'Do you know Long Wivutts, Robert?' she asked. 'It's a long way off the beaten track, a couple of miles the other side of Avecote. Patrick's rather in the dark as to its history.'

The name was vaguely familiar to Robert Conway, but he couldn't remember anything about the house. 'Why not ask at the next meeting of the history society?' he suggested. 'Someone there may know about it. Or try the library.'

Next day the promised rain arrived in full force, and it was pouring down as Hester, with umbrella aloft, dashed through the puddles to the county library, which had once been a gaming house in Regency days. All efforts to replace it with a modern building had been sternly rejected by the local council, much to the relief of the citizens of Chastlecombe. Which meant that the polished wooden floors and overhead beams and the gallery that girdled the upper floor lived in surprising harmony with the computers which had replaced the rubber stamps and filing systems of former days.

Hester made her request, then followed one of the librarians to the section on historic houses and began to search. It took quite a time, since Hester kept getting sidetracked by works which featured some of the great houses of the area. But eventually she ran to earth a slim volume, written fairly recently, about the histories of lesser-known local houses built in the sixteenth century.

Hester ran a finger down the index and gave a crow of satisfaction when she found that Long Wivutts had originally been known as Revel House, and featured in the last chapter in the book. Sternly resisting the urge to sit down and read then and there, she hurried to have the book checked out, thanked the librarian, and collected her umbrella. She arrived back at the shop out of breath, to find that Sheila had called David from his lair to deal with the one solitary customer in the shop.

'Hello, Hester,' said Patrick Hazard, smiling.

'Good morning,' she returned, aware of David's smug smile. 'What's brought you into town in this weather?'

'I spent the day alone at Long Wivutts yesterday,' he said. 'And it finally hit home that I can no longer inhabit an empty house with any degree of comfort. So I'm here to buy furniture.'

'I'll leave you in Hester's hands, then,' said David, grinning. 'Unless you'd like a look round the workshop before you go?'

'I would, very much,' said Patrick promptly.

'He'll probably put it in a book,' warned Hester.

'As long as he mentions Conway's in his dedication, I'm happy,' said David, and left them to it.

'What exactly do you have in mind?' asked Hester, then smiled in sudden excitement as she recalled the book in the damp carrier bag she was still holding. 'Just guess what I've got in here!'

'You've robbed the bank?'

'No, the library.' Hester took out the book like a conjurer producing a rabbit.

CHAPTER FIVE

'THERE'S a chapter on Long Wivutts,' she told him with triumph.

Patrick seized it with gratifying curiosity. 'Have you read it?'

'No. I had to dash back here. You take it,' she offered nobly.

'I've got a better suggestion. Have dinner with me tonight and we can read it together.' He paused, thrusting rain-darkened hair back from his forehead. 'Or are you booked up today, too?'

'No.' She smiled at him so warmly his eyes narrowed. 'If you like you can come to supper with me at my place. Then we can read it in peace, untroubled by waiters and other people's curiosity.'

'A tempting thought. Though I do tend to feel like the skeleton in the closet,' he admitted dryly. 'Are you ever going to appear with me in public, I wonder?'

Her smile faded. 'Of course if you prefer to go out somewhere, I really don't mind.'

'I was teasing, Hester.' He smiled into her eyes. 'I'm not idiot enough to turn down a meal alone with you.'

'I wonder why that sounds so dangerous?' she said flippantly, then smiled at Sheila as she rejoined them. 'I'm going to tempt Mr Hazard into buying up our entire stock, Sheila.'

'Then take all the time you like,' said Sheila, smiling back. 'I'll see to the rest.'

'What there is of it on a day like this!' Hester turned to Patrick purposefully. 'What exactly do you want me to show you?'

Her unexpected client, it seemed, wanted comfortable chairs and sofas for his sitting room, and some free-standing bookshelves.

'Obviously we only carry a small display in the actual shop,' said Hester, at one point. 'The rest of the stock is in our warehouse at the top of the road behind the market hall. And I can also provide you with brochures and catalogues to order from if you don't find anything to suit.'

'I need the sitting room stuff pretty urgently. I get tired of spending all my waking hours in the study or the kitchen.' He pointed to a pair of sofas covered in heavy, biscuit-coloured linen. 'I like those.'

By the time Patrick Hazard was finished he had bought the sofas and splurged on a dining room table and chairs made by David.

'Thank you,' she said warmly, then eyed him searchingly. 'But I do hope you didn't feel obliged to buy your furniture here. I wouldn't have taken offence if you hadn't.'

'Good,' he said, smiling crookedly. 'Because I've seen a pair of tapestry chairs I lust after in the antiques place down the road. You won't cast me off for ever if I buy them?'

'Of course not,' she said, smiling. 'I know the chairs you mean; they're perfect for Long Wivutts. Between you and me, Patrick, they've been there a while. Haggle a bit and you should get a good price— especially on a wet Monday morning!'

'Curtains?' he asked hopefully.

Hester shook her head regretfully. 'We don't do

those. But there's a shop in the arcade with wonderful fabrics, and they'll make them up for you.'

It was almost midday when Hester took Patrick to the resin-scented chaos of David's workshop. She left the men to it and went back to help Sheila with a sudden influx of visitors who were obviously more interested in sheltering from the rain than making any purchases. But after such a rewarding morning Hester was in such good spirits that she managed to pass them on to the group of rain-bedraggled tourists.

'Well,' said Sheila, after the last one had departed. 'I didn't expect any joy from that lot.'

Hester grinned. 'Presents to take home to the family.'

'The mood you're in, you could have sold snowballs to an Eskimo! I've brought sandwiches, by the way. So if you want to celebrate with David at the pub, I'll be fine.'

'I may, at that,' said Hester gratefully. 'What would we do without you?'

A few minutes later David emerged from the workshop with Patrick. 'How about taking our new customer out to the pub for lunch, Hester?'

'Good idea!' she said promptly. 'Just give me a minute.' Actually it was a brilliant idea, she thought, elated, as she hurried to the cloakroom to make repairs. Appearing with Patrick in public for the first time with David was the best arrangement possible. She frowned, aware that she hadn't roped David in the first time she'd gone out with Tim, or one of the others. But Patrick was different.

The hour spent in the King's Arms passed by so quickly that Hester eyed the clock with dismay.

David, following her glance, got up but put a firm hand on her shoulder.

'Drink your coffee in peace; Patrick will keep you company. I'll take over until you get back.' He took the hand Patrick stood up to offer. 'Thanks again for the order. Perhaps you'd like to come round to us for a meal some time. My wife's a great cook.'

'I'd like that,' said Patrick with sincerity. 'Thanks for lunch.'

'Our pleasure,' said David, grinning. 'It's not every day of the week we make such a killing.'

Patrick sat down, watching as David hurried off, greeting people right and left as he made his way out of the bar. 'He's popular.'

Hester nodded. 'David's always been an outgoing type. Yet he's perfectly happy shut up for hours in his workshop.'

'But I'm glad he deserted it for an hour today. This was a very good idea,' said Patrick, his tone suddenly very different as he looked at her. 'Here we are, Mrs Conway and the stranger, breaking bread together in a public place, with the official sanction from your brother-in-law to give us blessing.'

'It had occurred to me,' she said candidly. 'It was a good idea of David's.'

'It was *my* idea,' he contradicted smugly. 'David merely insisted on paying, due to my lavish expenditure in your emporium.'

'What it is to possess a devious mind!'

'Not devious. Just clever.'

Her lips twitched. 'But not modest.'

Patrick leaned back in his seat, eyeing her. 'So, Hester. Have you repented of your rash invitation this morning?'

'No. But leave it until about eight, if you don't mind. Give me time to make the meal.'

'We could send out for something.'

'But we're not going to,' she said firmly. 'I asked you to supper, so supper you shall have. Any allergies? Dislikes?'

'No allergies, and I doubt you're likely to serve me tripe, or pig's trotters!'

Hester shuddered. 'No, indeed. Nor organs, as my mother calls them—liver and kidneys and so on.'

'Highly nutritious, Hester,' he said reprovingly.

'Not if it makes the cook so nauseous she can't eat them.'

Patrick laugh. 'Next time you eat with me I'll get Mrs Wilf to make rabbit stew again.'

Hester pulled a face. 'Please don't. I can't bear the thought of rabbit, either.'

'You're very hard to please!' He paused, eyeing her. 'Which is true, actually. I was astounded by the invitation to supper.'

'I was a bit surprised myself.'

He smiled quizzically. 'Not something you do much?'

'No. The only men I invite to Pear Tree Cottage are Robert and David.' Hester flushed, and his smile widened.

'Don't worry, Hester. I shan't leap to rash conclusions.'

She got up. 'Time I went back. I've traded on Sheila's good nature long enough for one day.'

Patrick rose and collected his caped raincoat, then accompanied her out into the square. Hester put up her umbrella and smiled at him.

'See you tonight, then.'

'I shall look forward to it,' he said quietly. 'Thank you, Hester.'

'It's I who should be thanking you for your magnificent order, Patrick. Goodbye for now.'

Hester hurried over the slippery cobbles to the shop, bracing herself for David's teasing.

'I like your new friend, Hester,' said David, surprising her. 'I don't suppose you've got any other secret admirers ready to spend a packet here?'

'He's not a secret admirer.'

'Very true—he's pretty open about it.' And with an outrageous wink David took himself off.

The rain stopped shortly afterwards, and the sun began to break through, bringing some customers into the shop—for which Hester was grateful, since it prevented any temptation to read about Long Wivutts. The house belonged to Patrick; he was entitled to read about it first.

On the way home Hester made a swift foray through the local food shops, then set about marinating chicken breasts in olive oil with lemon rind and crushed garlic, prepared vegetables and pared apples, then simmered the latter in spiced butter while she whisked round with a duster and vacuum cleaner.

After the sketchiest tidying-up she ran upstairs and took a shower, then pulled on brown velvet trousers and a baggy rose-pink sweater. She did her face swiftly but took care with her mouth, applying a pencil and lipstick the same shade of pink. She thrust her still damp hair through one of her collection of ribbon scrunchies, and ran downstairs to make the pastry which would transform the apples into *tarte tatin*. When it was in the oven she laid the table, then sat down for a moment, breathing like a marathon runner.

Wine, she thought in sudden panic. Patrick drank wine and she didn't have any. Nor would he bring any because he knew she didn't like it. Frantically she rummaged in the cupboard under the stairs and found a six-pack of the lager she kept for David. She thrust the cans in the refrigerator, then put the vegetables to cook while she seared the chicken on her griddle. At two minutes to eight everything was transferred to dishes in the warming oven, and at precisely eight o'clock the doorbell rang and, flushed and slightly breathless, Hester opened it to greet Patrick.

'Hello again,' he said, his green eyes warm with approval, and presented her with a perfect white hydrangea in a blue porcelain pot. 'Since I couldn't bring you wine I thought you might appreciate this. I was assured that you could plant it in the garden later.'

'How lovely. Thank you. Come in.'

Hester's front door led directly into the room which took up the entire original ground floor of the cottage, with a staircase which led directly from it to the floor above. The conservatory-style kitchen had been added to the cottage at a later date.

Patrick looked round with interest at the touches which gave character to the room—the copper pot of flowers on the wide stone hearth, the *famille* rose bowl on the deep window-ledge, a vivid landscape glowing on a plain white wall. 'This is a very welcoming room, Hester.'

'Thank you.' She smiled. 'But I'm not giving you time to linger in it. And I'm afraid beer is all I have to offer you—I forgot to get any wine. The meal is ready, so would you mind coming straight to the kitchen?'

Patrick sniffed the air appreciatively as he sat down at the small kitchen table. 'Something smells good.'

Hester whipped dishes from the warming oven to the table, peeped into the oven and turned it off, then sat down to serve her guest with the aromatic chicken. 'Sorry there's no first course. I didn't have time.'

'Hester,' he said emphatically, 'I came here for the pleasure of your company. Not,' he added, after tasting the chicken, 'that my taste-buds are disappointed. This is wonderful.'

Relieved, Hester began to eat her own dinner, and they talked easily together on a variety of subjects including their tastes in literature.

'Talking of which,' said Patrick, accepting a second portion of chicken, 'have you peeped into the book yet?'

'Certainly not,' she said loftily, then grinned. 'But I was tempted. Fortunately I was too involved with the meal to have time.'

'I should have taken you out somewhere,' he said, frowning. 'You're a busy lady, Hester. I wasn't thinking when you offered to cook tonight.'

'I always used to when Richard was alive—and I had a far bigger house,' she said quickly. 'And Richard had a vast appetite. He taught me to cook, by the way.'

'Is this one of his recipes?' asked Patrick, eyeing his plate.

'Oh, no. He liked roasts and meat pies and that kind of thing, and loathed garlic. I hope you don't. I saw this on television the other day.' She smiled. 'You're my guinea-pig; I've never done it before.'

Patrick's eyes gleamed. 'I love garlic. You can experiment on me any time you like.'

'Rash of you, Patrick. Another time it might be inedible.' She took their plates and bent to take the tart from the oven.

'As long as there *is* another time I'll risk that,' he said with emphasis, his eyes holding hers as she sat down again.

After a pause Hester occupied herself with serving him a slice of tart, more pleased by his remark than she cared to admit. 'It should be proper custard instead of cream with this, but time didn't allow,' she said carefully. She was enjoying herself, she realised as she began on her own pudding. There were so many solitary suppers in her life these days that it was pleasant, more than pleasant, to have Patrick Hazard for company.

'This,' he said, mouth full, 'is superb, custard or no custard. Don't tell me this is the first time for the pie, too?'

'No. I make it a lot. It's Robert's favourite.'

'Robert?'

'My father-in-law.'

'Ah, yes.' Patrick laid down his fork, challenge in his eyes. 'But you don't cook for your other followers?'

'Followers! That's an old-fashioned word.'

'But apt. They follow, by the sound of it, but they never catch you.'

'Perhaps they don't want to.'

'Or perhaps they're waiting for you to stop mourning your dead husband.'

Hester regarded him levelly. 'You don't pull your punches, do you?'

'The truth may hurt, but it's sometimes necessary.'

'And you always deal in the truth?'

Patrick shrugged. 'I try to. I loathe deceit. One thing I must say for Alicia—she was honest about her feelings for Jay Benedict from the start.'

'Good for Alicia,' said Hester, secretly irritated. 'More tart?'

'Yes, please.' He grinned. 'I shall persuade myself I'm not greedy by refusing cream this time.'

After the meal Hester flatly refused to let Patrick help with the dishes as he wanted to. 'No, thanks, I'll do that after you're gone.' She smiled a little. 'I don't allow guests to wash up.'

'I thought you didn't entertain any here.'

'I meant Robert, David and Tally and the women-friends I invite round for pasta and chat sometimes. My mother, I admit, ignores my veto.' Hester waved him ahead of her to the parlour. 'Take a seat while I make coffee—which, I warn you, is only instant.'

Afterwards, the coffee drunk, Patrick turned to her with purpose. 'Right, then, Hester—no more suspense. Let's get at the book. You read, I'll listen.'

Hester curled up on her usual chair by the hearth and reached for her spectacles from the small table piled with books at her elbow.

Patrick leaned back on the sofa, his lips twitching. 'Ah, the lady Justice of the Peace.'

'That's me. Are you ready?'

'Oh, yes,' he said very softly. 'I'm ready.'

Hester shot a stern glance at him but he smiled innocently, and after a pause she began to read.

Long Wivutts had been built in the mid-sixteenth century in the characteristic local style, which the author described in much detail. Hester read through it hurriedly to find that the owner had been a merchant who'd made his fortune in the cloth trade, and had originally intended a much larger house. But when Thomas Revel had lost his wife and family to the smallpox he'd abandoned his grandiose plans and contented himself with a modest dwelling which he shared with a second wife, and spent considerable sums on the church in nearby Avecote as a memorial to the first.

'I wonder what Mrs Revel Mark Two thought of that,' said Patrick dryly.

'"Land,"' Hester went on '"was hard to come by, as so much Cotswold land belonged to the church. Twenty roods was the most Thomas could acquire." How much is that?' she asked.

'Five acres. It's dwindled to just over two, now.'

'Pity.'

'You wouldn't say that if you had the job of clearing it!'

'I would, you know—I like gardening,' she assured him, then went on reading. '"Long Wivutts was handed down to descendants of Thomas until the middle of Victoria's reign, when a prosperous mill-owner bought it. His family continued in it until just before the Great War, when William Latimer—"'

'Latimer!' said Patrick, leaning forward.

Hester nodded, eyes sparkling, and went on. '"Lieutenant William Latimer, of the Gloucestershire Regiment, married the daughter of the house and began living there with his bride in 1913..."' she paused.

'What is it?'

'"He fell at the Somme in 1916,"' read Hester, clearing her throat. '"His wife, Grace, who had inherited her family's wealth, remained there for the rest of her life, alone, and died in 1980. Since then, up to the time of publication, the house has changed hands several times.'''

They looked at each other in silence.

'Why,' said Hester carefully after a while, 'has it changed hands so much?'

'Your friend Dan Raymond said most people found it too isolated.' Patrick shrugged. 'I never met the people selling it. They live in London, and bought Long Wivutts for a weekend retreat, but after doing up the kitchen and the bathroom they put it in the hands of the estate agent again. I gather it's been empty for well over a year.'

'You'd think people would *want* a weekend place to be peaceful and far from the madding crowd and all that,' said Hester, taking off her glasses. She looked at Patrick questioningly. 'Maybe they thought it was haunted. You and I both feel *something* there.'

He nodded. 'I grant you that. But Mrs Latimer doesn't walk the house at night weeping for the dead Lieutenant, I assure you. Or if she does I haven't heard her.'

'Perhaps she likes you better than the others.'

Patrick shook his head, smiling. 'I doubt it. But if she does she must like you, too.'

Hester shivered a little, and looked through the book again. 'I thought there'd be more details than this. Doesn't your Wilf know anything about Mrs Latimer?'

'Do you know, I never thought to ask! Dan Raymond just said she lived alone all those years, except for a maidservant and a man who helped in the garden—which, I gather, was the lady's main interest in life.' Patrick's eyes held hers. 'Maybe gardening was Mrs Latimer's therapy when she was widowed.'

Hester nodded. 'But she never remarried. Which is odd. She was young—also wealthy, by the sound of it.'

'But there was a dearth of young men after the war,' Patrick reminded her. 'The cream of the crop met their death in the trenches. There were a lot of widows around in those days, so she probably had no choice. Unlike you,' he added deliberately.

She refused to be drawn. 'Talk to Wilf—or, better still, ask his wife.'

'I will.' Patrick leaned forward and took the book from her hands. 'No more history lessons tonight.'

'Just as well,' said Hester gloomily. 'It's my turn to give a talk at the history society tomorrow. Battles fought locally in the Civil War—Royalists and Roundheads and all that.'

'Your favourite period in history?'

'It's certainly one I know most about.' Hester leaned over to pick up the typed speech to show him, then sat very still as Patrick's hand touched hers. She turned her head to meet his eyes, and tensed at the look she met there.

'Hester,' he said very softly, 'have you any idea how much I want to make love to you?'

'No.' She breathed in deeply. 'And I hope you won't try to show me. I haven't—I mean I've never wanted—'

'To make love with anyone since Richard?'

She nodded. 'Believe me, I've tried. But it was a disaster.'

'Perhaps both timing and man were wrong.'

'Maybe.' Hester looked at him squarely. 'But I

think it's something more fundamental than that. I like you, Patrick, and I feel comfortable with you. Most of the time. But I probably misled you by inviting you here tonight.'

'You mean you can't bear the thought of making love with me?' he asked conversationally.

'Or with anyone else, if that makes it more palatable.'

'Not much.' He smiled, and shook his head. 'Don't worry, Hester. It's not a problem. We shall stick to pure, platonic friendship if that's all you have to offer.' He raised an eyebrow. 'I assume this is familiar territory for you—covered before with the others?'

'Actually, no.' Hester smiled bleakly. 'None of the three you have in mind has ever tried to get me to bed. The fiasco was with someone else entirely. He looked on me as a challenge.'

'Foolhardy man,' murmured Patrick, and got up. He held out his hand to pull Hester to her feet. 'When shall I see you again?'

'You still want that?'

He took her by the elbows and shook her slightly. 'I like being with you, Hester, and of course I want to make love to you—what man wouldn't? But I'm not so callow as to forgo your friendship if that's the only thing available to me. On the other hand,' he added, 'you may change your mind one day.'

'And if I never do?' she asked swiftly.

'Never's a long time, Hester.' He smiled, touched a finger to the tip of her nose and went to the door. 'How about braving Chastlecombe society at the Assembly Rooms on Thursday? It's a Mozart concert.'

She pulled a face. 'Sorry. Edward's taking me to that.'

'Hell—dinner on Saturday, then?'

'Sorry again. I'm going to the dinner I didn't get to last Saturday. I couldn't refuse Annie Raymond again.'

'Why not? You refuse me all the time!' Patrick wagged a finger at her. 'Tomorrow you're addressing the history society. Wednesday I'm having dinner with Lydia and Jack. Thursday you're a concert-goer. Is Friday any good?'

She nodded, smiling. 'Yes.'

'Good. And this time,' he added menacingly. 'I'm taking you out to dinner—will you, nill you, fair maiden.'

'As you wish,' she said, batting her eyelashes demurely, and suddenly Patrick caught her in his arms and kissed her on both cheeks.

'Goodnight, Hester. Thank you for the meal. I'll call for you about eight on Friday. And don't wear the black dress.'

CHAPTER SIX

AFTER Hester's lecture to the history society she spent a celebratory hour with Annie Raymond over a salad in the local wine-bar.

'Fascinating talk, love,' said Annie, who was an elegant forty-something with determinedly red hair and a very kind heart. Her only flaw, from Hester's point of view, was a yearning to see her young friend established in a new relationship of some kind. 'I trust you are definitely coming on Saturday? My freezer is bursting with the food I had to stuff in it after last week's cancellation.'

Hester assured her she hadn't the nerve to say no a second time.

'Good,' said Annie, and fixed Hester with a glittering dark eye. 'You still haven't told me why you said no the first time.'

'I had a previous engagement.'

'I *know* that. I want to know who with.'

'Patrick Hazard,' said Hester, resigned.

Annie frowned. 'The man who bought that old house out at Avecote?'

'That's the one.'

'I thought he was married. No? What's he like?'

A good question. 'Very nice,' said Hester guardedly.

Annie's eyes sparkled with curiosity. 'How did you meet him?'

'He bought some of David's pieces for his house. David likes him.'

'Do *you* like him?'

'Of course, Annie. Otherwise I wouldn't have gone out with him.'

'Where did you go?'

Dangerous ground. 'We drove quite a long way— one of those riverside places. Very pleasant.' Hester got up decisively. 'I really must go. I didn't have time to water my plants before I came out.'

Annie jumped up and kissed her cheek. 'All right, working girl. I know you get up early. Not that it does you much harm—you look positively blooming these days.'

Did she? Hester walked home through the summer twilight, deep in thought. It was pointless trying to deny that Patrick Hazard had brought an added zest to her life lately. Obviously it showed. She wondered where Patrick was going to take her on Friday.

She shrugged as she turned down the quiet road to Pear Tree Cottage. It was no big deal. She dined out regularly with Tim or John. Edward was more inclined to concerts and the occasional arty film beforehand, but all her engagements involved a meal in public. It ought to be no different with Patrick. Yet it was.

There was a message waiting for her when she got home. Hester felt a leap of pleasure at the sound of Patrick's voice. 'You're late, Hester. You ought to be home by now. Ring me tomorrow.'

Hester disciplined herself to wait until the following evening before her call, as a treat to look forward to after a busy day. During the afternoon Edward rang to apologise. He'd come down with the bug that was going round and couldn't make it to the concert, but would send the tickets round to the shop.

'Try someone else,' he said, coughing. 'I don't think it's Tim's cup of tea, but John might take you.'

Or I might possibly go alone or not go at all, thought Hester irritably when she put the phone down. It was obviously taken for granted that her spare time would be divided between the three friends, as though the arrangement was a permanent one. A respectable four-sided triangle—which, Hester informed herself, was a square. And very square she would become if she didn't watch out.

'Can I have the brochures for that new bedroom furniture?' said Iris, coming into the office. 'Dear me, you look belligerent. Someone ruffled your feathers?'

Hester grinned. 'Yes, a bit.' She hunted out the brochures. 'Fancy a couple of tickets for the concert on Thursday?'

Iris shook her head ruefully. 'Not me, dear, thanks. I'm strictly a country and western fan.'

Sheila, though fonder of classical music, was due at a parents' evening at her son's school that night.

'I don't suppose you want a couple of concert tickets?' Hester asked David later.

'No fear. What's on?'

'Mozart. Edward Moore was taking me, but he's caught the local bug.'

'One bar and I'd be snoring,' said David with a grin. 'Sorry.'

Hester decided to give the concert a miss and deposited the tickets at the Assembly Rooms box-office on her way home. She went to bed relatively early that night, after an evening which was oddly restless—due mainly to the fact that when she'd finally allowed herself to ring Patrick she'd been obliged to leave a message on his machine.

She was propped up against pillows with a novel, deep in the intrigues of the Jacobites—who'd tried to put the Pretender, James Stuart, on the throne to oust his cousin George of Hanover—when the telephone jolted her back to the present.

'Hello,' she said cautiously, looking at the clock.

'Patrick,' said the familiar, clipped voice. 'Sorry it's late. I just got in. Did I wake you?'

'No. It's not *that* late.'

'Are you in bed?'

'Yes.'

'Alone?'

'No.' There was a pause. Hester could almost feel the shockwaves coming through the receiver. She relented. 'I'm in the company of a crowd of Jacobites all plotting to restore the Stuarts to the English throne.'

'1715 or 1745?' he asked, without missing a beat.

'The period following the rebellion, such as it was, of 1715. I think of Bonnie Prince Charlie's later efforts as ''the Rising''.'

'You did that on purpose,' he accused.

'I know. Sorry.'

'When,' he went on with deliberation, 'you do share your bed with someone, Hester, make no mistake—it will definitely be with me.'

She swallowed, her pulse suddenly faster. 'You're very confident.'

'Faint heart never won fair maiden, and so on.'

'Why are you ringing, anyway? Is Friday off?'

'Certainly not. I just rang up for a chat.'

Hester smiled involuntarily. 'At eleven-thirty at night?'

'I rang earlier last night but you were out, and tonight I've only just got home from my sister's place.'

'How is she?'

'She looks exhausted. Jack was being horribly cheerful all night to hide how anxious he is.' He sighed. 'I don't know how a man copes at a time like this. He told me he feels so bloody helpless.'

Since Hester had no experience in this particular matter she had no opinion to give. 'I hope everything goes well for her,' she said with sincerity.

'So do I.' He changed the subject abruptly. 'How about dinner at Bredecote Hall? I hear the restaurant there is pretty good.'

'I don't know; I've never been there.'

'I hoped you hadn't. It's a good twenty miles away, so I'll pick you up at seven.'

'I'll look forward to it.'

'So shall I. Goodnight, Hester.'

'Goodnight.'

'Sleep well.'

'I usually do.' Hester put the phone down, smiled at Richard's photograph and put the light out.

'Did you enjoy the concert last night?' asked Patrick as he drove her through the warm summer evening on the way to Bredecote Hall.

'I didn't go. Edward's down with this flu that's going round. I asked around, but no one fancied a night of culture so I left the tickets at the Assembly Rooms.' Hester smiled at him. 'Pity, though. I like Mozart.'

'Why didn't you go alone, then?'

The confident tones were more clipped than usual,

and, thought Hester, frowning, held a sudden tinge of hostility. Why? She glanced at him curiously. Patrick looked rather wonderful in a fawn-coloured light-weight suit, his face dark against the white of his shirt collar. And she wasn't looking too bad herself, in the pink shantung dress which had caught his eye at Mrs Cowper's. Her hair was loose and shining, and she'd taken a long time to make up her face to look as natural as possible. But her escort was suddenly and all too obviously in a bad mood.

'I did some gardening instead.'

'I would have been happy to take you to the concert. I suppose it never occurred to you to offer *me* the spare ticket?' said Patrick, overtaking a lorry with rather alarming panache.

'No,' said Hester breathlessly. 'It didn't—could you slow down a bit, please?'

'Why?'

'I scare easily—'

'I meant why didn't you ask me?'

Hester chose her words with care. 'You saw me last Saturday, and again on Monday, and we were due to go out again tonight. Even if I'd thought of it, which I didn't, it would have seemed like overkill.'

His jaw set ominously. 'I see.'

'Look,' said Hester angrily, 'if this is your mood for the entire evening I'd rather go back home right now.' She saw his hands clench on the steering wheel, the knuckles white for an instant, then the car slowed perceptibly and she sensed his effort to relax.

'Sorry, Hester. I'm behaving like a schoolboy,' he said at last.

'Yes, you are,' she agreed, and to her relief he smiled reluctantly.

'I still think you couldn't face going out with me to such a public place,' he said bluntly.

'You're wrong. I never even thought of asking you.'

'That's supposed to make me feel better?'

She laughed. 'Sorry, Patrick—oh, how lovely!'

Their argument was forgotten as Patrick turned off the road down a long, formal drive where wildfowl strutted on the grass and more sailed on the large lake which came into view in front of a building more in the style of Queen Anne than the earlier architecture common to the Cotswolds. The sun set the water on fire as Patrick parked the Jeep among more elegant vehicles drawn up on the tree-fringed space near the pillared main doors.

'A good thing I didn't wear jeans tonight,' said Hester later, in the large conservatory which housed the bar.

Patrick moved a little closer on the sofa they were sharing. 'Not that you didn't look good in them, but tonight you look perfect for your surroundings,' he assured her.

'So do you.' She toasted him with the glass of Pimm's he'd insisted on. 'May the rest of the evening pass without—friction.'

'Amen to that.' He smiled, his eyes green as the manicured grass of the lawns outside, and suddenly Hester felt absurdly happy—glad to be sitting in this beautiful place with attentive waiters and a lively buzz of conversation from the other diners. It was a beautiful summer evening, she knew she was looking good and her escort was easily one of the best-looking men in the room.

The feeling persisted as they ate exquisitely pre-

NO COST! NO OBLIGATION TO BUY!
NO PURCHASE NECESSARY!

PLAY "LUCKY 7"
AND GET AS MANY AS FIVE FREE GIFTS...

HOW TO PLAY:

1 With a coin, carefully scratch away the gold panel opposite. Then check the claim chart to see what we have for you – FREE BOOKS and gift – ALL YOURS! ALL FREE!

2 Send back this card and you'll receive specially selected Mills & Boon® novels from the Enchanted™ series. These books are yours to keep absolutely FREE.

3 There's no catch. You're under no obligation to buy anything. We charge nothing for your first shipment. And you don't have to make any minimum number of purchases – not even one!

4 The fact is thousands of readers enjoy receiving books by mail from the Reader Service™. They like the convenience of home delivery and they like getting the best new romance novels at least a month before they are available in the shops. And of course postage and packing is completely FREE!

5 We hope that after receiving your free books you'll want to remain a subscriber. But the choice is yours – to continue or cancel, any time at all! So why not take up our invitation, with no risk of any kind. You'll be glad you did!

You'll look like a million dollars when you wear this lovely necklace! Its cobra-link chain is a generous 18" long, and the beautiful puffed heart pendant will add the finishing touch to any outfit!

The Reader Service™
FREEPOST
Croydon
Surrey
CR9 3WZ

NO
STAMP
NEEDED

sented food in a room more like a library than a dining room, with books on floor-to-ceiling shelves on some walls, beautiful panelling on others and the only lighting—other than the sunset glow from the windows—coming from candles in silver holders. Enclosed with Patrick in such intimacy, with only the occasional intrusion from a waiter, Hester smiled at him in the candlelight, her pleasure in the occasion open on her face.

'This was an inspired choice, Patrick. Thank you for bringing me here.'

'I thought its distance from Chastlecombe might be the best thing going for it, but I was wrong.' Patrick glanced around him. 'I haven't come across better service or food anywhere, certainly not allied with surroundings like these. Jack was right.'

'He's brought your sister here?'

'Not yet. He came to a conference recently, and recommended it.'

The earlier clash was forgotten. The evening proceeded in complete harmony as Hester reported on her talk to the history society, and Patrick on his progress with the book. They had savoured the leisurely meal and repaired to the conservatory again, to drink coffee and watch the moon rise over the lake, before he reverted to their earlier disagreement.

'I'm sorry I was angry,' he said at last, taking her hand as they sat together near the windows to enjoy the view.

'Why did you mind so much?' she said curiously, watching his slim fingers as they smoothed the back of her hand.

'Because I'm vain, I suppose. It was a bit deflating to learn you never even thought of asking me to the concert, Hester. On the other hand I value truth. I would like us to be the kind of friends who are totally honest with each other, always.'

She eyed him wryly. 'I wouldn't have been asked to sit on the bench if I wasn't known to possess a certain amount of integrity, Patrick. But nobody's perfect.'

He smiled. 'True.'

'And are you always unfailingly honest? Do you never lie, Patrick?'

'I suppose if you asked me if I liked your dress, or the way you'd done your hair, I might possibly say yes even if I didn't mean it, to avoid upsetting you. But on important issues I try to deal in the unvarnished truth.'

'You were pretty blunt about the black dress!'

'But that was because of what it represented.'

Eventually they went outside into the moonlit night, where a rim of afterglow still lingered on the horizon. Stars were appearing and the evening was still, and Hester breathed in deeply as they wandered back to the car.

'This is an outrageously romantic place, Patrick.'

'I know,' he said smugly. 'Why do you think I brought you here?'

She looked at him and laughed. 'A softening-up process?'

'Yes,' he said shamelessly. 'I'm doing all I can to establish myself in your good books: buying furniture from you, ingratiating myself with your family— David, anyway. And,' he added, his voice deepening, 'I'm somehow managing to keep at arm's length when you know perfectly well my instincts urge me otherwise. In the interests of truth I'm warning you—it's all a plan of campaign.'

They stopped outside the car in the shadow of an overhanging tree.

'Campaigns usually mean battles,' she said thoughtfully. 'What, exactly, do you intend to gain?'

'Victory,' he said promptly, and took her in his arms and kissed her.

Hester stayed very still in his embrace, her mouth unresponsive. Then deep inside her she felt stirrings of long-dormant response. Of its own volition her body curved against his, her lips parted and she felt a shudder run through him. His chest rose and fell more rapidly, and her own breathing accelerated to match. He drew her closer, then a group of departing diners emerged from the hotel entrance and the spell was broken.

Patrick let out a deep, unsteady breath and released her with gratifying reluctance. He unlocked the car, lifted her into the passenger seat, then paused with his hands either side of her waist as he looked deep into her eyes. 'I wish I hadn't kissed you, Hester.'

Her eyes opened wide. 'Why?'

'You know why. Now I shall never be able to rest until I've kissed you again.'

'That would be a pity,' she whispered, and leaned forward until her lips touched his. 'There. Is that better?'

'No,' he said with sudden violence. 'It's not.'

The drive home was accomplished in silence, Hester taut with expectation of what might happen at the end of it. Patrick glanced at her from time to time, but the entire twenty miles passed without a word of conversation, until every nerve in Hester's body felt winched to snapping point. When they arrived at Pear Tree Cottage Patrick killed the engine, helped her out and walked with her to her front door, holding out his hand for her key. He unlocked the door, stood back for her to go inside, then followed her in and pulled her into his arms, his back against the door.

The kiss was an explosive mixture of desire and release from the tension which had built between them during the long drive. Patrick slid his hand down her back and splayed it at the bottom of her spine, moulding her against him, and Hester trembled at the contact as though she were a schoolgirl and this her first experience of the changes desire wrought in a man's body.

When he raised his head at last Patrick looked pale beneath his tan, as though the self-control he was so patently exerting was costing him dearly. 'I'm going home,' he said roughly, in a voice so hoarse and far removed from his normal, confident tones that Hester clenched suddenly chattering teeth.

'Would you like coffee?' she said with difficulty.

'No, I wouldn't,' he snapped. 'You know damn well what I want, so I'm taking myself off before you throw me out. The entire evening was one long, aphrodisiac experience from start to finish. If I'd known the effect that hotel would have on my libido I'd have given the place a wide berth. So goodnight, Hester.'

'Goodnight, Patrick.' She pulled herself together. 'Thank you for—for a beautiful evening.'

For a moment she was sure he was going to seize her in his arms again, but instead he turned blindly and went out, slamming the door shut behind him.

Hester stood where she was until she heard him drive away. Then she went upstairs, stripped off the dress and took a shower, got into bed and lay looking at Richard's photograph in silence.

When the phone rang she realised she'd been waiting. She let it ring three times, then picked it up.

'Hello.'

'I thought I'd ring to say goodnight, Hester,' said Patrick in her ear.

'Thank you. I'm glad to know you're home safely.'

'Are you?'

'Yes.'

'Then I didn't blot my copybook irreparably?'

'No, Patrick.'

'Good. Sweet dreams, then.'

He rang off, with no mention of another meeting. Hester smiled a little in the dark.

Having roused a response to her, Patrick was unlikely to leave matters there. Nor, she realised, did she want him to. It had been good to feel the old, familiar heat rush through her, to know that her normal, healthy female responses were no longer dead. Patrick was the first man since Richard to arouse the least flicker of response in her. Which added an exciting sensual nuance to the mental accord she'd experienced with Patrick almost from the first.

Her smile widened. In the past she had sometimes envisaged meeting someone else once she'd got over her grief for Richard. But never in her wildest dreams had she imagined the encounter would happen in court.

CHAPTER SEVEN

NEXT day the weather remained bright and hot, and summer visitors swelled the usual crowd of Chastlecombe weekend shoppers. Conway's was as busy as the rest of the town. Their impressive choice of furniture was the bedrock of the business, but Hester's display of porcelain and pottery and various other small items like footstools and elegant waste-paper baskets were popular as suitable gifts, or merely as mementoes of a holiday to take home. By the time the shop closed that evening all members of staff were very glad to finish work.

'Are you out socialising again tonight?' yawned David as he went round setting the alarms.

'Yes,' said Hester without enthusiasm. 'Dinner party at the Raymonds'.'

'Do I detect a note of ennui?'

'Not really. An hour in the bath and I'll be fine.'

David saw Iris and Sheila off the premises, with much teasing about Saturday night debauchery, then came back to Hester. 'Right. Tell all. I know you went out somewhere with Patrick Hazard last night. Tally's agog, so give me the details.'

Hester obediently gave an edited account of the dinner at Bredecote Hall.

David whistled. 'Extravagant devil, isn't he? Was it as good as its reputation?'

'Better.' Hester collected her belongings. 'It's your anniversary soon—take Tally there. It's wonderful.

Four-poster beds and whirlpool baths and so on.' She giggled at his raised eyebrows. 'I looked through their brochure.'

He grinned. 'After all that it's a bit of a comedown tonight, then, dining with Annie and Dan.'

'Certainly not.'

'I suppose your Three Musketeers will be there?' David locked up with his usual care then lingered with Hester, looking at the window display for a moment before going off to his car.

'Two of them, yes,' she said, with a sigh. 'I just wish Annie could bring herself to invite odd numbers for a change. I get fed up with being paired off with whatever spare man she can rustle up.'

The Raymonds lived on the outskirts of town in a modern house skilfully designed to blend with the local architecture, with an acre of garden surrounded by high laurel hedges. Hester had been rather more tired than usual at the end of her Saturday. After dawdling in the bath longer than intended she arrived late, to find all the other guests assembled on the lawn at the back of the house in a buzz of conversation and laughter, glasses in hand.

Annie, red hair recently touched up, all her warpaint in place, greeted Hester with a hug—looking, for Annie, somewhat nervous. 'You know almost everyone, of course. Come and let Dan give you a drink, then I'll introduce you to the new faces.'

Most of the faces were indeed familiar, including those belonging to Tim Galbraith and John Brigham. The former promptly provided Hester with a tall glass of non-alcoholic fruit punch in return for a kiss on the cheek, but Annie swiftly detached Hester to introduce her to the couple the Raymonds had met on a golfing holiday in the Algarve.

'And I believe you know Patrick Hazard,' went on Annie, avoiding Hester's eyes. 'He's bought an old house out in the wilds beyond Avecote somewhere.'

Hester said all the right things, chatted to the newcomers, drew Patrick into the conversation and did her level best to be the perfect guest. But it was difficult. Not only was she furious with Annie for springing the surprise on her, she was also bedevilled with vivid memories of the embrace she'd shared with Patrick the night before. And unless her antennae were badly out of kilter she felt sure Patrick was thinking the same thing.

Later it came as no surprise to find herself seated beside him at one of the tables on the terrace when they were bidden to eat. While the cold gazpacho was served Hester managed a private word under cover of the general conversation going on around them.

'I didn't know you were coming,' she muttered, shaking out her linen napkin.

'I left a message on your machine,' he returned in kind, and met her eyes for an instant.

'I was in a rush,' she said, flushing. 'I forgot to look.'

Dan Raymond leaned between them to place bottles of wine on the table. 'Help yourselves. You know Patrick already, I believe, Hester?'

'Yes. He's bought some of our furniture for Long Wivutts.'

Dan nodded genially. 'He rang me this afternoon about records for the place but I couldn't be of much help, I'm afraid.'

'At which point,' said Patrick in an undertone when

Dan had gone, 'Mrs Raymond, who had picked up the extension, interrupted to ask me to dinner.'

'Did she now? At such short notice she was lucky to find you available,' murmured Hester, and sipped the fruit punch Tim had topped up before he took the other seat beside her.

'Actually I was going over to Lydia's for a meal tonight, but I cried off once I had the chance of dining here. Or, to be more precise, the chance of seeing you again. Which is the object of the exercise.' And with a polite smile Patrick turned away to talk to his other dinner partner, leaving Hester to the mercies of Tim Galbraith.

Tim was a very handsome man. And very aware of it. But for once he was not the centre of attention at the party, and he plainly resented it. He became determinedly proprietorial towards Hester, discussing the changes he'd helped her plan in her garden, in very audible tones, and generally behaving as though she'd been invited solely for his entertainment. Hester, usually able to parry his overtures with ease, found it oddly difficult with Patrick seated beside her, his leg pressed very deliberately against hers under the table. He was dressed in much the same way as the night before, his appearance so obviously appealing to the lady on his right that Hester wanted to scratch the woman's eyes out.

Good heavens—she was jealous. For a moment it was difficult to recognise the emotion. Richard had never given her cause for jealousy. But, to be fair, Patrick wasn't giving her any, either. At which point Tim was obliged to turn away from her to talk to the lady on his left and Patrick bent down to retrieve his napkin. Fiery heat ran through her as his fingers closed round her bare ankle for a moment. Then he straightened and turned to smile into her eyes.

'Have you had a busy day, Hester?'

'Very,' she managed with difficulty. 'And you?'

'I've spent most of it slaving in the garden. Wilf says this weather's going to break by Monday.' He waited for a moment while they were served with salmon mayonnaise, then added, 'I've got some news. About Mrs Latimer.'

Hester smiled at him in delight. 'Really! What is it?'

'I'll tell you later when I take you home.'

Hester gave him a brief, quickly veiled look of such radiance that he turned away abruptly and drank some wine, leaving her to the mercies of Tim again.

The evening was wearing from that point on, since Annie was determined to steer Hester into Patrick's company all night and Tim was equally determined to detach her from it. He stuck to her like glue when the party retired inside after dinner, bringing her more fruit cup she didn't want, standing over her while she drank it and generally behaving as though she belonged to him. Hester controlled her growing irritation by concentrating on the fact that Patrick was taking her home. But after a while she began to feel hot and dizzy, and grew more anxious to go home by the minute, whether Patrick accompanied her or not.

At last she met Patrick's eyes across the room, escaped Tim's clutches by pleading a visit to the bathroom and buttonholed Annie in the hall.

'It was a lovely party but I'm a bit tired, Annie—'

'I must be off, too,' said Patrick, joining them. 'Thank you for a delightful evening, Mrs Raymond.'

He turned to Hester. 'Are you driving, or can I give you a lift?'

'Hester walked here,' jumped in Annie quickly. 'I'm sure she'd appreciate a ride home.'

'Thank you, I would,' said Hester, who was beginning to feel quite strange. 'Goodnight, Annie; I won't interrupt Dan. Say thank you for me.'

'Of course, love.' Annie kissed her cheek and shook Patrick's hand, looking very pleased with herself as she reiterated how glad she was he'd been able to come. She opened the door for them just as Tim Galbraith came into view, looking like a tiger baulked of its prey, whereupon Annie almost thrust them outside and closed the door on them in haste.

Patrick seized Hester's hand and ran with her outside into the road, where the Jeep was parked at the end of a line of cars. Once they were on their way he met her eyes and both of them began to laugh helplessly.

'Subtlety isn't Mrs Raymond's strong point, is it? Does she do this to you often?'

'Throw me at her male guests, you mean?' asked Hester, her head reeling in a highly disturbing manner. 'All the time. She's very kind-hearted, and she means well.'

'Since she was throwing you at me tonight, I agree. But I wanted to punch Galbraith in the nose,' he added abrasively.

Hester bit her lip. 'I don't know what got into him. He's not usually such an idiot.' She put a hand to her head, swallowing hard.

'What's the matter?' said Patrick swiftly, glancing at her.

'I feel a bit odd. Funny—I kept to the fruit punch all night.'

'You're not coming down with this bug that's going round, by any chance?'

She shook her head, then groaned, regretting it. 'If I didn't know better I'd say I'd had too much to drink.'

'Let's get you home,' he said tersely, and within minutes the Jeep was at the gate to Pear Tree Cottage. When she unfastened her seat belt and tried to get out Hester found her legs refused to obey her. Patrick demanded her key, then lifted her down and supported her up the path, his arm round her waist. When they were inside the cottage Hester broke away from him, swaying, and clapped her hands to her mouth, her eyes wide with horror.

Without a word Patrick picked her up and raced upstairs to the bathroom, then held her head while she parted with her dinner. Hester gasped and heaved for what seemed like hours, tears streaming down her face, too wretched for embarrassment. When the paroxysm was over at last Patrick ran water into the bath, pulled the zip down on the back of the black dress he disliked so much, made sure she was steadier on her legs, then left her in privacy.

Twenty minutes later Hester appeared at the top of the stairs, her face a perfect match for her white towelling dressing-gown. Patrick sprang up the stairs, hands outstretched, but she gave him a wobbly smile.

'I can get down under my own steam—I think.'

'Take my hand,' he ordered.

Hester obeyed, feeling her way down the polished wooden stairs with bare feet, glad of the warm clasp of his fingers.

Patrick led her to the sofa. 'I foraged and made you some tea.'

Hester's heavy eyes lit up. 'Perfect. Just what I need.'

'Feel better now?'

'Yes. A lot. My head's not reeling any more.' She smiled ruefully. 'I must have eaten something. Yet we all had the same thing, and you seem to be all right.'

Patrick handed her a cup and saucer, then sat down beside her. 'But I didn't drink any fruit punch.'

Hester frowned. 'It was just Annie's usual thing. She always provides it for what she calls the "dutiful drivers".'

'And you kept to it all night?'

She nodded. 'It tasted a bit different, now I come to think of it—maybe some of the fruit was a bit iffy.'

Patrick shook his head, his eyes grim. 'Or Galbraith doctored your drinks.'

Hester stared at him. 'But surely I'd have tasted any alcohol?'

'If it was vodka, and he did it cleverly enough, you probably wouldn't notice much difference.' He touched her hand. 'Does Galbraith sometimes take you home after this kind of thing?'

'Yes. Or John. And sometimes I drive myself. There's no hard and fast rule.'

'I think Galbraith had plans for you tonight, Hester.' Patrick's smile was wry. 'Once he met me, anyway. My presence annoyed him—the stranger in town trespassing on his property.'

Hester put the cup down on the tray with a crash. 'I am not Tim Galbraith's property, nor does he want me to be. I've told you, Tim's a friend. He knows the rules.'

'Very possibly. But I think he fancied breaking a couple tonight. He didn't like it when I sat by you at dinner, or that we already knew each other. Suddenly Mr Dog-in-the-Manger wanted to snap.' Patrick slid his arm round her and pulled her against him comfortably. 'Is your dislike of alcohol well known?'

'Well—yes, I suppose so. People I see regularly know I don't drink much. Lady magistrates aren't expected to,' she added with a smile.

'Then he was sure a slug or two of vodka would soften you up towards him on the way home. He was obviously intending more than a peck on the cheek tonight.'

'If so he got it a bit wrong—I could murder him!' She sighed, her face suddenly hot as she remembered the unpleasant interlude in the bathroom. 'With a contrast to yesterday evening. Sublime to the ridiculous with a vengeance. I'm sorry, Patrick.'

'I'm not,' he said lazily, rubbing his cheek against her hair. 'What are friends for?'

'I'd rather they weren't obliged to hold my head while I throw up!'

'Nonsense. It's brought us closer together.' He moved suddenly, releasing her to shift along the sofa. 'But you must be wanting to get to bed.'

Hester felt oddly bereft. 'Which means that you are,' she said with regret.

'Yes, I am. But not in precisely the same context.' His eyes met hers. 'In fact,' he added deliberately, 'my thoughts run to bed far too much when I'm with you, Hester.'

Colour returned to her pallid face with a rush. 'Do they?' she said steadily.

He breathed in deeply. 'Normally, I warn you, I

would have taken that as an invitation. In the circumstances I'll be noble and take myself off.'

'But you were going to tell me about Mrs Latimer!'

'So I was. What are you doing tomorrow?'

Not for the world would Hester have admitted that she'd deliberately kept her Sunday free. 'Nothing very much. I thought I'd just potter about in the garden.'

'Compared with my garden yours looks like an entry for the Chelsea Flower Show,' he said, getting up. 'Come and potter in mine with me instead. Mrs Wilf has left me a casserole to heat up, so lunch isn't a problem.'

'If I don't come I don't hear about Mrs Latimer?'

'Right.'

'I thought you said you were noble.'

'In certain circumstances I can also be ruthless,' he assured her.

'I believe you.' Hester shrugged. 'All right, then. I'll drive over about twelve.'

'Not before then?'

'No—chores to do first.'

Patrick leaned down, holding out his hand. 'Up you come. You still look pale—which gives me the excuse for this.' He picked her up and carried her up to her bedroom, laid her on the bed and stacked the pillows behind her. 'Can I get you anything else?'

She shook her head. 'Would you put the lights out? The front door will lock automatically behind you.'

Patrick nodded, then leaned down and kissed her mouth gently. Her arms went up around his neck and with a sharp intake of breath he gathered her close and kissed her fiercely, then let her go and straightened, smiling at her ruefully. 'I didn't mean to do that. Goodnight, Hester. Sleep well.'

'Goodnight, Patrick—and thank you.'

He brushed a hand over her hair and turned to go, then paused, looking at the photograph on the dressing table. 'This is Richard?'

'Yes.'

Patrick gave her a wry look. 'Only one photograph?'

'What did you expect—a shrine? When I moved here the object of the exercise was to make a life without him. But I couldn't banish him altogether.'

Patrick eyed the photograph dispassionately, then went to the door and turned to look at her. 'Tomorrow, then. No later than twelve.'

Hester smiled. 'On the dot. Goodnight.'

After the stresses and strains of the night Hester slept late next morning and woke, refreshed, to another day of sunshine and a strong sense of happy anticipation. She arrived at Long Wivutts just as a church bell somewhere was pealing midday. Patrick came out to greet her, looking very different from the elegant city lawyer of the night before. He was stripped to the waist and wore mud-encrusted jeans and army boots. He was also dripping with sweat, and put out his hands to keep her at a distance.

'You're punctual and I'm a mess. Sorry, Hester. How do you feel?'

'Surprisingly well,' she assured him.

'You look it. Come and sit in a deck chair and direct operations while I finish digging a border Wilf wants to plant up. What's this?' he added as she gave him a cardboard box.

'My contribution to lunch.'

'That's very good of you. And in this state I can't

even give you a brotherly peck of appreciation by return.' Patrick waved her before him into the welcoming house and closed his impressive front door on the world. In the kitchen he opened the box, licking his lips when he saw the newly baked fruit pie. 'What's in it. Apples?'

'Peaches and apricots.'

'A lady of many talents!'

Hester gave him a curtsy only slightly marred by her jeans. 'I've come to help. I've got a change of clothes in the bag, so I'm quite happy to get dirty.'

'In that case shall we postpone the casserole to dinner time and just have a sandwich for lunch?'

'Am I staying to dinner, then?'

'Of course you are.'

Hester grinned. 'Give me a minute to change and I'll be with you.'

'I thought you were changing afterwards!'

'No, indeed. This is my Sunday best.'

Upstairs in Patrick's bedroom Hester stripped off her jeans and pink cotton shirt and pulled on khaki shorts and a yellow vest, old tennis shoes and a green-lined white cotton cricket hat.

'Very businesslike,' said Patrick when she joined him at the far end of the lawn. 'What's in the rucksack?'

'Gloves, trowel, fork and secateurs.'

'I do have some garden tools,' he informed her with dignity.

She smiled. 'I'm sure you do. But these are special—my mother gave them to me when I moved into the cottage. I'm used to them. So let's work.'

Hester was as good as her word. An hour later, when Patrick called a halt, only a moderate stretch of herbaceous border had been released from its prison of weeds but progress had definitely been made. To her amusement Patrick resorted to a hammer in places to break up the rock-hard clay.

'Wilf's little tip,' he said, grinning. 'I'm going in for a shower before we have lunch. So up you come.'

Hester glanced at her watch. 'I'll just finish this bit first. Call me when you're ready.'

Patrick went into the house, whistling, and Hester laboured on, so absorbed in her task it seemed like only minutes before she felt his hand under her elbow—and this time, protest as she might, she was forced to give in and go inside.

'Oh,' she said, looking at the kitchen table. 'You've made the sandwiches, too. I was going to do those.'

Patrick, who was now rather more respectable in a plain white T-shirt and some shorts similar to Hester's, gave her five minutes to wash. 'Then come and have a drink. Orange juice, water—?'

'Water, please,' she said with a slight shudder. 'After last night I'm off fruit juice.' She kicked off her grubby tennis shoes and ran upstairs to the bathroom to wash her sweating pink face. A vast improvement on last night, she informed it, and hurried downstairs in bare feet, so much at home in the house she was beginning to take the feeling for granted.

They ate cucumber sandwiches with hunks of crumbly Cheshire cheese, but Hester shook her head when Patrick cast covetous glances at the pie.

'You won't feel like work again if you do,' she warned. 'Let's keep it for supper.'

'Were you a prefect in school, by any chance?'

'Oh, yes. I was a schoolmarm too, remember?'

'But with nice young ladies for pupils!'

'Some of them were proper little handfuls, I assure you.' Hester got up to fill the kettle, then bit her lip. 'All right if I make some tea?' she said over her shoulder.

'My house is yours, Hester. Do exactly as you want.' Patrick leaned back in his chair, watching her, long brown legs crossed at the ankles.

'I had some mad idea I could clear that border in two days, you know,' he said, laughing at himself. 'A city slicker like me had no idea what hard work it is just to do some simple weeding.'

Hester leaned against a counter while she waited for the kettle, giving his slim, muscular frame a top-to-toe scrutiny. 'You don't *look* like my idea of a city lawyer, actually.'

'Why not?'

'Too fit.'

'My original law firm provided the staff with an in-house swimming pool, gym and squash court, and when I changed jobs I ran a couple of miles every morning before work,' he informed her, then grinned. 'And since I arrived here I keep in condition with a couple of hours in this garden of mine before I sit down at the computer.'

She nodded. 'It's been left to run wild for a long time. Which reminds me—you promised to tell me about Mrs Latimer,' she reminded him. 'We can't get back to work until our lunch goes down, so talk.'

Patrick sat forward and leaned his elbows on the table. 'Mrs Wilf, would you believe, is a niece of one Miss Lily Deakin—she who was Mrs Latimer's general factotum from the mid-thirties until Mrs Latimer died in 1980.'

'*Really?*' Hester's eyes lit up. 'Where is she now?'

'Alive and well, with all her faculties in good nick, and living in sheltered accommodation in Avecote.'

'I know the place,' said Hester instantly. 'Pretty little bungalows with a hotline to a warden. How old is Aunt Lily?'

'Late seventies—but bright as a button, according to Mrs Wilf. Auntie would be only too happy to talk about Mrs Latimer any time we want.'

'It's you who must talk to her,' said Hester swiftly. 'It's your house.'

'I'll talk to her alone the first time, perhaps.' Patrick took the transistor outside so that they could listen to an orchestral concert on Radio Three while they laboured in the afternoon sunshine, but when the concert ended Patrick called a halt. 'That's enough, Hester. It's your day off—and you were very unwell last night. I'd forgotten that.'

'I'm glad.' She pulled a face, then eyed the cleared strip of border with satisfaction. 'That, Patrick Hazard, looks a lot better.'

'Thanks to your invaluable efforts. We make a good team, Hester.' He collected her bag of tools and waved her in front of him. 'Go up and have a bath. Afterwards we can loll about out here in deckchairs while the casserole heats up. It's a pity to go indoors in this weather.'

'Amen to that. I won't be long.' Hester ran upstairs and stood under a hot shower, helping herself to some herbal shampoo. Afterwards she towelled her hair dry, brushed out the tangles, ran her fingers through it a few times then secured it with one of the ribbon scrunchies she carried with her at all times. Wrapped in a towel, she went back into Patrick's bedroom, dressed in the pink shirt and jeans and thrust her feet into her flat navy leather loafers. Then she slapped moisturiser on her flushed face, put some lipstick on, packed her grimy clothes in her small holdall and went downstairs to Patrick, who was reading the Sunday papers which were spread out on the kitchen table.

'Your turn,' she said briskly.

'You were quick!'

'The sunshine's too good to miss,' she assured him. 'I'll have tea ready when you come down.'

By the time Patrick returned, in immaculate chinos and a cream poplin shirt, Hester had taken the newspapers and the tea-tray out into the garden, and was sitting in a deckchair, her glasses on, reading book reviews.

They drank tea and ate the last of Mrs Wilf's fruitcake, Patrick deep in an article on a famous crusading Queen's Counsel, Hester absorbed in the magazine section, and after a while Patrick went in to switch the oven on, ready for their evening meal.

'What a wonderful, glorious day,' he said with satisfaction, and sat down again beside her.

'We were lucky with the weather,' she agreed. 'My days off are all too often wet.'

'I wasn't referring to the weather,' he said, taking her hand.

Hester's heart missed a beat. She fixed her attention on the trees in their early summer greenery, at the splashes of crimson and pink from clusters of peonies and the delicate white of syringa. 'When you've got it in shape this will be a heavenly garden. But shouldn't you be grafting away at your book instead of out here?'

'I make it a rule to work a five-day week—in

weather like this, anyway. If it rains, and I feel like working on a Sunday, then obviously I do.' Patrick stretched luxuriously, his hand tightening on hers. 'But I would much prefer to spend all my Sundays exactly like this. With you.'

weather and the forsythia... something... and their first
weekend in... Sunday... then afterwards... for... But it
all came beautifully, Just then the insistence of mine was...
none... would probably prefer... at the... Sunday... some
over the sudden... the house...

CHAPTER EIGHT

HESTER sat very still. Every Sunday? She stared down
at the hand holding hers, astonished by a sudden im-
pulse to kiss the white scratches on the sun-browned
skin.

'I've obviously rendered you speechless,' he said
dryly. 'Don't panic. I'll settle for the Sundays you can
spare—for the time being.'

She turned her head to meet the eyes which looked
so darkly green under the tree, a match for the leaves
which rustled slightly in a rising evening breeze. 'For
the time being?'

He nodded. 'If I demand too much, too soon, I
might frighten you off.'

'Why do you think that?' she said casually.

Patrick let out a deep breath. 'Because so far in our
acquaintance I've worked hard, proceeding inch by
careful inch into your favour. This is not,' he said,
smiling crookedly, 'my normal practice with a
woman.'

'Then why with me?'

To her surprise he got up, pulling her to her feet.
'Let's discuss it later. After we've eaten.'

Burning to continue the discussion there and then,
Hester went without argument into the house, where
Mrs Wilf's casserole was scenting the air. She put her
peach and apricot pie on the top shelf of the oven to
warm, then, suddenly hungry, helped Patrick lay the

table, accepting a handful of peanuts from him as they worked.

'I seem to eat a lot of meals with you lately,' Hester remarked, munching.

Patrick grinned and took mineral water from the refrigerator for the table. 'Not nearly enough.'

She smiled at him happily, and paused in the act of distributing knives and forks. That was it, of course—she felt happy with Patrick. Happier than she'd ever thought to be again.

They ate the lamb casserole with hunks of bread, then demolished half the fruit pie, talking about Patrick's research and the latest commission David was fulfilling.

'You never discuss your days in court,' said Patrick, helping himself to more pie.

'No, never.'

'Do you enjoy being a magistrate?' he asked curiously.

'I don't think ''enjoy'' is the right word,' she said slowly. 'Some of the cases we try are so pathetic I used to feel very depressed at first. But one develops a shell after a while. Every week I deal with problems which put my own in perspective.'

'And do you have many problems, Hester?'

'Doesn't everybody?' Her eyes narrowed ominously. 'I think Tim Galbraith is beginning to be one of them—I shall have words with him tomorrow.'

Patrick's face hardened. 'You're seeing *him* tomorrow.'

'Yes. I ordered some plants from him; he told me last night they'd arrived. I'll take the car tomorrow and pick them up on my way home.'

His face cleared. 'Perhaps I should pick them up for you and have words with him myself.'

'No way. I fight my own battles.' Hester smiled to soften her words. 'But thank you, Patrick.'

After the meal was cleared away they went outside to sit in the garden and admire the evening. This time Patrick took her hand as soon as they sat down, and Hester lay back, relaxed, liking the feel of the hard palm, callused from labours with spade and hoe, warm and protective against hers. They talked desultorily for a while, at ease with each other to such an extent that after a while they lapsed into comfortable, companionable silence.

There were rustles in the shrubbery and more in the trees as the breeze grew bolder. The light was just beginning to fade from the sky, and after a while Hester felt the slim fingers tighten on her own. Dreamily she turned to meet the eyes which had been watching her all the time.

Patrick got up and pulled her gently from the chair. With a sigh of pleasure she leaned against him. He locked his arms round her and she slid her own round his waist, her cheek against his chest, his chin against her hair. He removed the ribbon, running his fingers through her hair, and she lifted her face to receive his kiss.

'It was your mouth I noticed that first day,' he murmured against her parted lips. 'Madam Justice sitting here with never a hair out of place, slanting gold eyes hidden behind those ridiculous spectacles of yours. But nothing could disguise your mouth. Very discreet lipstick, as befits a lady magistrate, but even so I thought of sunripe peaches and warmth and this—'

He kissed her again, and Hester responded with a

lack of reserve which took his breath away. He crushed her close and she locked her hands at the nape of his neck, giving him back kiss for kiss. And suddenly, breathing hard, he took her by the hand and drew her with him into the house.

'Come and sit on my knee in the study. Could you hurry up my furniture delivery? I don't even have a sofa yet,' he groaned. 'My house isn't fit for you, darling.'

'You've got a bed,' Hester pointed out gruffly, then went scarlet to the roots of her hair, as startled by her words as he.

'Not inch by inch any more?' he demanded, eyes blazing, and she shook her head. Hand-in-hand they went up the stairs to his bedroom, where the breeze brought scents of summer through the open window, adding to the welcome Hester felt so strongly in every part of Patrick's house. He closed the door behind them, then took her in his arms again and held her close, his mouth hungry on hers as he caressed her with unsteady hands.

With one arm tight around her waist, as though he couldn't break contact for an instant, he bent to strip back the covers from the bed. Then they were kissing again, wildly, their shaking, urgent hands discarding clothes in frantic haste as they sank down together in a tangle of entwined limbs, straining each other closer.

Patrick kissed her mouth and her breasts, then turned her over and laid kisses down her spine before turning her back to kiss her mouth again. She returned his caresses with mounting fervour, and at last, astonished, heard herself utter a hoarse little plea.

'Not yet,' he breathed against her mouth, and

clasped her hands and moved them high and wide, looking deep into her eyes. 'There will never be another time like this—the first time for you and me.'

A shiver of pure delight ran through her and she lay still, seeing herself mirrored in the eyes which desire had dilated almost to black.

'Patrick,' she said huskily. 'I've never had a lover since—but you know that.'

He nodded, strands of bright hair falling across his damp forehead. 'I hoped.'

'Why?'

He shrugged, and she thrust herself closer instinctively, felt him tense. 'I knew from the start that you were different.'

She looked at him questioningly. 'And you?'

'No one for a long time—and never any more, Hester,' he said simply, and kissed her, pushing her hands wider until she felt abandoned and vulnerable beneath him, shaken to find herself deeply aroused by the sensation. 'You,' he added, against her mouth, 'are what I've subconsciously looked for since the day I saw Alicia and Jay fall in love before my very eyes. I never thought it would happen to me.'

Hester turned her head away. 'You don't have to say you're in love with me,' she muttered. 'For this, I mean. I know you like me—'

'*Like* you!' Patrick closed his eyes for a moment, then turned her face back to his and kissed her savagely—and suddenly the lull was over. No comparisons, some last, small functioning part of her mind warned her, and she abandoned herself to him, glorying in the subtlety and tenderness he was capable of for a surprisingly long interval before he was overwhelmed by fierce, demanding need which aroused an answering wildness entirely new in Hester's experience.

For a long time afterwards they lay entwined and utterly still except for the rise and fall of their slowing breathing. When Patrick moved at last it was only to pull up the covers and hold her closer, and after a while, bemused and utterly happy, feeling she was where she belonged, Hester fell asleep in his arms.

'Darling,' said a voice in her ear, and Hester stirred, muttered crossly, and tried to burrow back into the bare shoulder which had been her pillow.

'No good growling at me,' said Patrick, laughing softly. 'Come on, wake up, sleepyhead; it's after ten.'

Hester shot upright. 'I'll be late for work—oh!' She blinked, met Patrick's eyes and began to laugh.

'Ten at night—and all's well. For me, anyway,' he said, ruffling her hair. 'I'd like you to stay, but don't worry—I won't even ask.'

'I wish I could stay, too,' said Hester, surprised that she felt so self-conscious.

'You look as though you belong in my bed,' he told her, attuned, as usual, to her thoughts.

'I feel it, too,' she confessed, and pulled a face. 'But unfortunately it's time I went home to my own.'

'I suppose it is.' Patrick slid out of bed and began to dress. 'While you get yourself together I'll go down and make us some coffee.'

Hester smiled at him, grateful for his tact. 'Just give me five minutes.'

'Not a second more,' he ordered, and bent down to kiss her, then went from the room, whistling.

Hester washed and dressed hurriedly, brushed her hair and left it loose, then collected her belongings and ran downstairs and straight into Patrick's arms as he emerged from the study. He kissed her hard, and went on kissing her, and at last buried his face against her hair, breathing rapidly.

'Let's go in the study and drink our coffee in two separate chairs like Derby and Joan. Then you must go home.' He put her away from him. 'I should have come to collect you this morning. You shouldn't be driving alone on these country roads at this hour.'

'It isn't even properly dark yet,' she said reassuringly, and smiled pertly. 'And I promise to go straight home.'

'I should bloody well hope so,' he said, giving her a smack on the bottom, and she protested, laughing, and fled into the study.

While Hester poured the coffee Patrick drew the curtains and switched on lamps. And when they were sitting either side of the fireplace in the deep leather chairs he said abruptly, 'We must talk.'

She eyed him warily over the rim of her cup. 'What about?'

'Us.' He drank some coffee, then put the cup down and leaned forward, his hands clasped between his knees. 'Hester, I feel as though I've known you all my life—but to the rest of the world it would seem like unseemly haste if we went public just yet. Particularly with someone in your position.' He smiled at her possessively. 'On the other hand I intend to make it clear to all and sundry that from now on you're spoken for.'

Hester looked at him questioningly. 'So how are you going to do that?'

'I shall make it plain I mean business,' he said flatly. 'Dining out, going to concerts, attending charity events and whatever else you do here in Chastlecombe you do with me from now on. No one will be left in any doubt as to my intentions.'

She began to laugh. 'You're going to come courting?'

'I certainly am. I trust you've no objections?'

'No.' She smiled demurely. 'I rather like the idea.'

'I thought you might,' he said smugly. Then his eyes darkened. 'I intend to make matters clear to Galbraith and co, and anyone else who has designs on Hester Conway.' He held out his arms. 'Now, come here and sit on my lap and tell me how clever I am.'

She went willingly—so willingly that Patrick, intoxicated by this new, compliant Hester, was reluctant to part with her when she tore herself away at last.

'I wish you could stay,' he said huskily as they walked, arms around each other, to her car.

'So do I.'

'Ring me as soon as you get in,' he ordered.

'I will.' Hester detached herself reluctantly and got in the car, and Patrick bent to look at her through the open window.

'I'll pick you up at the shop at five-thirty tomorrow.'

So he meant it. She smiled at him radiantly. 'All right. I'll cook supper—'

'No. Tomorrow night we dine at the King's Arms.' He kissed her quickly, then withdrew his head, and with a sigh of regret Hester started the car and drove up the long, tree-shaded drive, waving an arm through the open window as she turned through the gate.

When she arrived home Hester frowned to see lights on all over Pear Tree Cottage, and went quickly up the garden path. Before she could put her key in the door it opened, and a small, familiar figure stood in the oblong of light.

'Hello, darling,' said Celia Lucas. 'I got the key from David and let myself in.'

'Mother!' Hester embraced the small figure warmly. 'Why didn't you let me know you were coming?'

They went into the cottage and closed the door, Celia's brown eyes bright with curiosity as they examined her daughter from head to foot.

'I didn't decide to until this morning. It seemed silly to drive from Dorset to Warwick and not call in here *en route*. Didn't you notice my car? Obviously not—where have you been all day? I've been ringing you since about twelve, Hester, but all I get are your dulcet tones on your machine.'

Hester went into the kitchen to fill a kettle, and her mother settled herself at the small kitchen table with the air of a woman determined not to move a muscle until she discovered all she wanted to know.

'I've spent the day with a new friend, helping clear the garden.'

'Is she nice?'

'Very nice, but it's a he. Have you eaten?'

'Never mind that,' said her mother impatiently. 'Who is this man? If he's new, he's obviously not one of those tame Romeos of yours.'

Hester giggled, and explained about Patrick, his house, what he did for a living, his appearance, clothes, age and every last detail her mother demanded.

'Sounds like quite a man,' said Celia at last, accepting a cup of tea. 'No, nothing to eat, darling—

I'm on a diet. Tally insisted on plying me with her version of afternoon tea. I couldn't refuse, but I'm not entitled to eat anything else until about Tuesday afternoon.'

'Oh, Mother! What on earth do you want to diet for?'

'I couldn't get into my one and only designer suit. It's cheaper to diet than buy another one—but never mind all that.' Celia eyed her daughter searchingly. 'You look different, love.'

Did it show? Hester stretched, smiling. 'I had a nice day.' Which was the understatement of the year.

'If this Patrick Hazard is responsible for the glow I'd like to meet him.'

'How long are you staying?'

'Can you put up with me until Wednesday?'

'Of course. Stay as long as you like,' urged Hester, meaning it.

Celia smiled lovingly. 'Thank you, darling. But Paris and Aggie are in kennels—I must get back on Wednesday to collect them.'

Paris and Agamemnon were Celia Lucas's pair of rough-haired terriers, two of the reasons why Hester saw less of her mother than she would have liked.

'In that case you can meet Patrick tomorrow, Mother. He's collecting me at five-thirty—heavens, I forgot. I must ring him.' Hester ran into the other room to pick up the phone.

'Where have you been?' demanded Patrick wrathfully. 'It can't have taken this long to drive home!'

'My mother was here when I arrived—surprise visit.' Hester bit her lip. 'So perhaps we could postpone our meal at the King's Arms for a while. She's staying until Wednesday.'

'Certainly not,' he said promptly. 'Invite your mother to dinner, too. I'll be glad of the chance to meet her.'

'She will be, too,' Hester assured him dryly. 'But be warned—she can be a bit forthright.'

'Good. I'll look forward to meeting her.' His voice changed suddenly. 'Darling, I've been sitting here, reliving our day, hardly able to believe it happened. How the blazes am I going to sleep tonight?'

'No idea. Same problem.'

'Any regrets?'

'None.'

'Good. See you tomorrow. You can give me a drink at the cottage before we take your mother out. I need time to ingratiate myself with her.'

'Somehow I don't think you'll need much. Goodnight, Patrick.'

Celia came into the room, smiling broadly. 'So when do I get to meet him, then?'

'He's taking us to the King's Arms for dinner tomorrow night!' Hester seized her mother in her arms and gave her a smacking kiss.

'Goodness,' said Celia, startled. 'He must be something, this Patrick of yours.'

'He isn't mine—' Hester stopped, thinking it over. He is, though, she thought with sudden, fierce possessiveness. Just let anyone try to take him away from me.

Celia sighed deeply. 'You know, darling, I never thought I'd see the day. I've hoped, prayed—but sometimes I thought you'd never look at another man.'

'It took a while to get over Richard,' said Hester, unoffended. 'I loved him.'

'I know you did.' Her mother frowned. 'But I always thought you should have made a clean break, moved away from here entirely, instead of carrying on in the business and buying yourself this place.'

'If I had I wouldn't have met Patrick,' said Hester, picking up her mother's suitcase. 'Come on; let's put some clean sheets on the bed.'

The upper floor of Pear Tree Cottage boasted a bathroom and two bedrooms. Hester's was a reasonable size but the other one minuscule, and when her mother came to stay Hester always moved into it herself, refusing to let Celia use the narrow little bed. They had the usual argument about it but Hester wouldn't listen, and at last the double bed was made up with fresh linen.

'I must get some sleep,' said Hester, with a sudden yawn. So she was tired after all—and had a good right to be. She coloured slightly. 'Would you like anything before I go?'

'No, thank you, darling,' said her mother absently, her attention on the dressing table. 'What happened to Richard's photograph?'

'Didn't you notice it downstairs on the desk? Oddly enough I took it down there only this morning.' Hester smiled ruefully. 'For a while, after he died, I used to talk to it every night.'

'I was afraid you did,' said Celia, frowning. 'It worried me.'

'It needn't any more. Things are different now.'

'Since when?'

Hester made no attempt at prevarication. 'Since I met Patrick.'

'This man is important to you, then?'

'Yes. In fact—' Hester gave her mother a triumphant little smile '—I rather think we got engaged tonight.'

CHAPTER NINE

PATRICK began the following evening—so he informed Hester—as he meant to go on. 'Starting right now,' he said when he drove her away from Conway's that evening. 'I believe you had some plants to pick up?'

Hester stared at him, then began to laugh. 'I see. Having made David's day by picking me up in full view of my staff, you now intend to ruin Tim's.'

'As thoroughly as I can,' he agreed smugly.

'Is that why you're wearing your hot-shot city lawyer uniform?'

The day was much cooler, with a hint of the promised rain in the air, and Patrick was resplendent in a dark suit of impeccable cut. 'Certainly not. I'm keen to impress your mother.'

'You will,' she assured him as they drew up at Galbraith Nurseries.

Tim Galbraith came to meet Hester with a smile which died abruptly when he saw Patrick, and after an exchange of forced pleasantries Tim handed over the promised shrubs and perennials. At which point Patrick pointedly insisted on paying for the plants, stretching Tim's hard-won *bonhomie* to the limit.

'One down,' said Patrick with satisfaction, once they were heading back for Pear Tree Cottage. 'Now for the difficult bit—charming your mother into believing I'm good enough for her daughter.'

Celia Lucas, however—ready for the occasion in a

violet linen suit, her bobbed, silvery hair gleaming—
quite plainly took to Patrick Hazard on sight. An avid
fan of the courtroom-thriller genre, she was soon talking to him animatedly about his book, and, with an
amused look at the two people she loved getting on
like a house on fire, Hester took herself off to shower
and change.

Because it *was* time she admitted she loved Patrick,
quite apart from being *in* love with him. And Patrick
would be surprised to learn that he had one thing, at
least, in common with Richard Conway—Hester re-
spected him. In addition to his obvious physical attri-
butes Patrick possessed integrity, and a certain *gravitas* of mind and brain which set him apart from the
majority of men she knew. He possessed a quality
she'd never thought to find again.

The evening at the King's Arms was a great success. The three of them talked as though Patrick had
long been one of the family, rather than someone
Hester had known less than a month. Patrick informed
them that Lydia, his sister, would like to meet both
ladies the next day, if they could spare the time.

'Perhaps you could drive round there with your
mother on the way home from work, Hester,' suggested Patrick, and smiled wryly. 'I am not bidden to
accompany you on this occasion.'

The evening notched up another success from
Patrick's point of view. While they drank coffee in
the bar afterwards Hester saw several people she
knew, some of whom were acquainted with her
mother and would note the pleasure Celia was taking
in Patrick Hazard's company whether they knew him
or not.

'That,' said Celia with satisfaction, when they were

back in Pear Tree Cottage, 'was a very pleasant evening. Thank you for dinner, Patrick.'

'I was very glad of the opportunity to celebrate,' he said deliberately, and smiled at a rather flustered-looking Hester. 'I assume you know I'm in love with your daughter, Mrs Lucas?'

'Since you ask me—yes.' Celia smiled wickedly.

'Do you think it's reciprocated?' he asked.

'It's not me you should be asking, Patrick!'

At shortly after eleven, after a respectable interval with coffee and conversation, Celia Lucas—who never went to bed before midnight—announced that she was tired and, if Patrick would forgive the limitations of age, she needed her sleep.

'Limitations of age, my foot,' said Hester, lips twitching when she and Patrick were alone. 'My mother's all of fifty-four.'

'And looks a lot less,' said Patrick, grinning, and took her in his arms. 'She knew I wanted this.'

Since Hester wanted it too, there was silence in the room for a while as Patrick sat down with her in his lap and proceeded to kiss her until her lips were swollen, her hair stood on end and her eyes wore a dazed look that he noted with deep satisfaction when at last he raised his head.

'How long are you going to keep me waiting, darling?' he said urgently. 'Put this place up for sale tomorrow.'

Hester blinked. 'Sell my house?'

He nodded. 'You've known from the moment you set foot in it that your home is at Long Wivutts.'

She looked at him thoughtfully. 'I thought you had a campaign of courting in mind.'

'I do. But I was thinking in weeks, rather than months.'

'Give me a little time to get used to the idea—' The telephone brought Hester off Patrick's lap in a hurry to pick it up. She said hello, listened for a moment, then handed it over to Patrick quickly. He shot to his feet, looking tense.

'Right, Jack,' he said crisply. 'No—don't worry. Tell Lydia I'll explain. I'll drive over to your place straight away.'

He handed the phone back to Hester, looking worried. 'Lydia's gone into premature labour. Jack's rushing her to the hospital now. I don't fancy going home, under the circumstances, so I'll go over there for the night, wait for him to get back.'

'Is Lydia all right?' asked Hester anxiously.

Patrick smiled crookedly. 'Enough to apologise for cancelling your visit tomorrow. She says she hopes to meet your mother next time she's in town.'

'Of course—how sweet of her to think of it at a time like this.'

'Lydia's quite calm, apparently—unlike Jack.'

Hester, who had a feeling that underneath the calm exterior Patrick was as panic-stricken as his brother-in-law, put her arms round him and hugged him. 'You'd better go then, darling. Only, keep me posted, please.'

'You called me "darling"', he said huskily, and kissed her.

'Don't you want me to?' she said, when she could speak.

'Of course I want you to—along with a great many other things I want, none of which I've time to discuss right now.' Patrick kissed her again, lingeringly, then let her go. 'Apologise to your mother. I'll see you tomorrow, some time. By the way,' he added, frowning, 'on Wednesday I'm going to London for a day or two to see my agent, editor and barber, to name but a few. I'll be back on Friday.'

'I'll miss you,' Hester said forlornly.

'Good,' he said, and kissed her again.

After he'd gone Hester went upstairs to find her mother deep in the thriller she'd bought on holiday.

Celia pushed her spectacles up her nose and smiled. 'Patrick's taken off very early, darling.'

Hester explained about the emergency in the Barclay household.

'Goodness, men are always so useless in these circumstances. I remember your father—but never mind that.' Celia eyed her daughter, making no comment on her dishevelled appearance. 'Let's talk about Patrick. He's an absolute charmer, Hester, and very much smitten with you.'

'Do you think so?' asked her daughter eagerly.

'Did you doubt it?'

'No. But it's nice to have a second opinion.' Hester gave her mother a wide, happy grin of the type Celia hadn't witnessed in a long, long time.

'So when are you two going to tie the knot?' Celia asked, clearing her throat.

'Patrick seems to be in quite a hurry—suggested I put this place up for sale tomorrow, in fact.'

Celia looked taken aback. 'Would you mind? I mean, do you fancy living in this house of his?'

'Almost, dear parent, as much as I fancy Patrick,' said Hester, and kissed her mother goodnight.

*   *   *

Early the following morning Hester heard a sound and shot out of bed to see the familiar Jeep at the gate. She ran downstairs and opened the door as Patrick strode up the path, pale and in need of a shave but so obviously jubilant that Hester let out a sigh of relief.

He rushed her inside, took her in his arms and kissed her very thoroughly before he said a word.

'Niece Joanna born at six this morning, no complications and mother and baby doing well,' he said at last.

'Oh, Patrick, that's such good news!' crowed Hester, and hugged him hard. 'I didn't get much sleep myself, so heaven help your brother-in-law. How is he?'

'Shattered. He just staggered home, looking like the wrath of God, but grinning all over his face, and wanting nothing more than a couple of hours' sleep. I know the feeling,' added Patrick ruefully, then looked up as Celia came down the stairs, wrapped in a familiar white towelling robe.

'Sorry to interrupt,' she said. 'But I'm dying to hear the news. Good news, by the look of it,' she added, since Patrick was grinning from ear to ear as he reported for a second time.

'Wonderful—now I'll go back to bed.' With a smile Celia whisked herself back upstairs, and Patrick took Hester in his arms again.

'Me, too. I don't suppose you'd consider coming back to Long Wivutts and going back to bed with me?' he asked hopefully.

'Certainly not,' she said severely. 'Some of us work for a living, you know.'

'Are you suggesting my composition of deathless prose is not a proper job?' he demanded wrathfully, and she giggled.

'Your words, not mine.'

'On the other hand,' he said with a sigh, 'it's about time I got on with it. Deborah, my agent, will have words tomorrow if I can't report at least a quarter of it under my belt.' He eyed her moodily. 'Shall I see you tonight?'

'Much as I'd like to, no. I need to spend some time with Mother—and you'd better get some work done. Give me a ring when you get back from London. Now, go home and get some sleep,' said Hester, and kissed him quickly, then gave him a push. 'And for heaven's sake drive carefully. You look tired.'

In spite of her mother's company, and her days in the shop and at court, Hester missed Patrick so much that she wondered how she'd existed before without him, and told him so during his nightly telephone calls. The confession provoked a passionately appreciative response which sent her to bed each night in a turmoil of longing that kept her awake for hours. Once her mother had departed for Warwick Hester felt even more lonely, and channelled her energies into her garden during the evenings to dispel the emptiness Patrick's departure had left behind.

After a rather longer and more wearisome session than usual in court on the Friday, Hester arrived home to find the Jeep parked in the lane with Patrick at the wheel, reading a newspaper. She waved, beckoned him in, then flew up the path to unlock the door, all her weariness forgotten as Patrick followed her inside and took her in his arms.

'Mmm,' he murmured, his lips roving over her face. 'I needed that. Badly.'

'So did I,' she said fiercely, and brought his lips back to hers.

'How have you been?' he asked at last, raising his head, then he smiled crookedly and began taking down her neat coil of hair. 'Madam Justice, I assume?' He slid her tailored grey jacket from her shoulders and began unbuttoning her blouse, then he stopped. 'No,' he said decisively. 'Not here. Come home with me.'

'Now?'

'Any reason why not?'

Hester shook her head. 'Give me a few minutes to shower and change and I'm with you.'

True to her word, Hester ran downstairs ten minutes later in a yellow cotton dress, her hair hanging loose, knowing her face was glowing and her eyes sparkling. Patrick stood at the foot of the stairs and held out his arms. She ran into them and gave him a long, uninhibited kiss, then leaned back and said very firmly, 'I'm hungry. Is there anything to eat at home?' She coloured at this slip and Patrick's eyes lit up.

'You see?' he said forcefully. 'You think of Long Wivutts as home already. So hurry up with your private arrangements, Hester. I want you installed there as soon as possible.'

'I'll see what I can do,' she promised.

'Good. Let's go food shopping, then we'll head for Avecote.'

They filled a trolley with food at the supermarket on the outskirts of town, including the basics for the type of meal Patrick yearned for—thick slices of ham to fry with eggs, tomatoes and mushrooms.

'The great British breakfast?' said Hester as she bought some salad greens to salve her conscience.

'I never eat breakfast,' he said, and grimaced. 'And I ate too much designer food in London. I want truckers' fare tonight.'

They opened up the house to the warm summer evening and talked incessantly of Patrick's trip, what Hester had done while he'd been away, how much Patrick liked her mother, and vice versa, and, of course, the new baby.

'I sent Lydia some flowers, and I've bought a present for Joanna,' Hester informed him.

'Lydia told me about the flowers,' said Patrick, slicing bread. 'I called in on the way back.'

'She's home?'

'Against Jack's wishes, but she came home this morning. And sends thanks for your flowers, and bids me ask you to lunch on Sunday week. By then she hopes to be more organised.'

'That's so nice of her. But won't she be too tired? I admit I'm dying to see the baby, but we could just make a short visit to do that.'

'No. She's thrilled about us, and wants to welcome you into the fold.' Patrick gave a sigh of relief as Hester set plates of sizzling food on the table. 'You were quick—wonderful!'

After the meal they wandered round the garden, impressed by the progress Wilf was making. And then, arms round each other, they went upstairs to Patrick's bedroom and surrendered to the urgency neither could keep at bay any longer.

'I thought,' said Hester, a long time later, 'that it wouldn't be like the first time.'

'It wasn't.'

'No. It was—better.'

Patrick smoothed a hand down her damp, flushed

cheek. 'I didn't enjoy my trip to London. I kept thinking about this. Of being here with you, every day—and every night. I never thought it would happen, Hester. I never dreamed I'd be so lucky.'

'Neither did I.'

'But you've been in love before.'

She sighed. 'That was different.'

'Why?'

'I was younger then. And you and Richard are two very different people.'

Patrick propped himself up on one elbow, looking down into her face. 'In what way?'

'He was a lot older, for a start, whereas you are—how old? A year or so older than me?'

'Thirty-six next birthday.'

'I thought so.' Hester looked up at him candidly. 'Do you really want to talk about this?'

He nodded gravely. 'Now the subject's come up—yes, I do.'

She breathed in deeply. 'Well, to start with, you and I feel like equals. We function on the same wavelength, I think.'

'I know we do,' he assured her.

'Richard was a lot older than me. Older than his years, in some ways. I'm not saying he was like a father to me, but, though he loved me with passion, there was always a certain indulgence in it, in his entire attitude to me—as though on major issues in our marriage he was making allowances for my youth.'

'Were you looking for a father-figure when you married him?' said Patrick, frowning.

'Not consciously. I could have been, I suppose. My own father died when I was small.' She shrugged.

'Richard decided he wanted me right from the first. I was—swept off my feet, to be hackneyed.'

'I wanted you the minute I saw you, too.' He ran a long finger down her cheek and throat, following a line which led down to the hollow between her breasts. He bent his head and kissed her there, then looked up into her eyes. 'How did you react when you first saw *me*?'

'I didn't allow myself any reaction,' she retorted breathlessly. 'I thought you were the twins' father!'

'Ah, yes, the devilish duo. I hope young Joanna turns out less of a handful.' Patrick moved over her, clasped her hands and spread them wide—and Hester lay very still, her heart performing somersaults, her eyes wide on his. 'I want you again,' he said abruptly.

His words were superfluous, since his body was already signalling its desires so urgently she began to breathe rapidly, her eyes lambent on his. He released her hands, and she wreathed her arms behind his tousled blond head and abandoned herself to the waves of sensation which came together, faster and faster, until the end came with a frenzy so overwhelming it left them staring into each other's eyes in awe.

The next week was busy, but Hester made no more visits to Long Wivutts. 'Until I move in for good,' she said to Patrick.

On the Saturday evening Patrick took her to dine at an inn much patronised by the smart set of Chastlecombe, and smiled into her eyes across the table in a way which stated his intentions to anyone who cared to look. And not a few people did.

Next day they went to lunch with David and Tally, and Robert Conway was there. After a certain natural awkwardness at first the lunch party went well, and Robert, in private, gave Hester his blessing.

And, though he protested, she refused to see Patrick every evening. During the time they spent apart she went to the history society or played tennis, just as she'd always done, and attended the sessions of additional training she undertook regularly in her capacity as a magistrate. And when John Brigham, the Clerk of the Court, asked if the rumours he'd heard were true, she smiled, but gave him no definite confirmation.

'Discreet, as always. But perhaps I'll have a word in Eddie Moore's ear.' His eyes twinkled. 'It might save him some embarrassment.'

Annie Raymond was over the moon during their usual get-together after the history society, convinced that her invitation to Patrick had been the sole factor in getting them together.

'You are together, I suppose? Officially?'

'Not officially,' said Hester firmly. 'Let's just say that for the time being I'm not seeing anyone else.'

While she was enjoying a sandwich lunch with David and Tally at the King's Arms next day Tim Galbraith came in, and, without asking, joined them at their table.

'Is it true?' he demanded, eyeing Hester belligerently.

'Hello, Tim, nice to see you,' said Tally pointedly, putting a hand on her bristling husband's arm.

Tim flushed. 'Sorry, you two. Forgot my manners.'

'We were just going,' said Hester, finishing her coffee.

'Stay for a minute, please,' he said urgently, and

eyed the other two in appeal. 'I just want a private word with Hester. Ten minutes.'

David looked at Hester questioningly. 'Is that all right with you, love?'

'I suppose so,' she said, openly reluctant.

Tally and David both kissed her rather deliberately before leaving Hester with Tim, who glared after them irritably.

'Did they think I was likely to make violent love to you in the bar of the King's Arms?' he demanded.

Hester sighed. 'Look, Tim, I need to get back to work fairly soon—'

'I won't keep you long,' he promised. 'Let me buy you a drink.'

'No thanks.' She relented slightly. 'Another coffee, then.'

When the cups were in front of them Hester looked very squarely into Tim's eyes. 'Talking of drinks, Tim, did you doctor mine at Annie's dinner party?'

He smiled uneasily. 'It was just a little joke, Hester. How did you know? I thought you wouldn't taste the vodka.'

'I didn't recognise the taste, certainly. I thought Annie'd put some different fruit juice in it. Why did you do something so stupid, Tim?' she added relentlessly.

He stirred a spoon round in his coffee, staring down into the cup. 'You've always been so damned self-possessed, Hester; I just wanted to loosen you up. You were always so bloody platonic with me. Like everyone else, I gave you time to get over Richard. But one day I thought we might make a go of it.'

'Oh, come on!' she said scornfully. 'That's nonsense, Tim.'

His head went up. 'Is it nonsense, Hester?' he asked swiftly. 'Are you serious about this Hazard guy? Because if you are you might like to know that he's in the habit of entertaining other ladies to lunch in remote little hostelries behind your back.'

Hester got up. 'I don't have to listen to this—'

Tim rose and caught her hand. 'This isn't gossip. It was my father who mentioned seeing him on Thursday. With some blonde, Hester.'

'His sister, probably—let go my hand.'

He obeyed, his lips tightening.

'I must go,' she said briskly. 'Goodbye, Tim.'

'I'm coming with you.'

And to avoid making a scene Hester had no choice but to let him.

'Are you sure there's no chance for me?' Tim persisted as he walked with her towards Conway's.

'None.' Hester came to a halt outside the shop door. 'There never was. I'm sorry you thought otherwise. Though personally, Tim, I don't think the idea ever occurred to you until Patrick came on the scene. And,' she added, 'just to make things perfectly clear, I can't forgive your puerile trick of spiking my drinks. I'm a magistrate, Tim, and I try to behave like one. You could have made me drunk in public, and I resent that deeply. If your idea was to make me amorous towards you it went wrong. Your little scheme just made me sick. In more ways than one.'

CHAPTER TEN

AFTER a sleepless night, with Tim's spiteful little story ringing in her ears, Hester found Patrick rather abstracted during their Saturday evening together. Since she had more right to be distant she was annoyed, and almost—but not quite—decided against asking him in when he drove her back to Pear Tree Cottage after a meal in an unpretentious little pub she'd introduced him to.

'Did you like the Cherry Tree?' she asked as she made coffee.

'Yes, I did,' he returned, watching her from the kitchen doorway.

'Thought you would.'

'Now why,' he added slowly, 'do I detect some significance in that statement?'

'You've obviously got a taste for obscure country pubs.' Hester dumped two mugs of instant coffee on the kitchen table and sat down at it, eyeing him with sudden, overt hostility. 'You told me you hadn't been anywhere this week.'

'I haven't. I've been slogging away at my computer.' Patrick frowned and took the chair opposite. 'Get it off your chest, Hester. What's bugging you?'

'I might ask you the same question,' she snapped. 'You've been like a polite stranger all evening.'

He looked at her morosely. 'I was waiting for you to tell me something.'

Hester frowned. 'What, exactly?'

'Why you lied.'

'When?' she said, astonished.

'When I rang you last night you told me you'd had lunch with David and Tally.'

'I had!'

Patrick shook his head. 'I called in the shop yesterday, on the off chance of finding you. That lad of yours—Mark—directed me to the King's Arms, where I found you deep in conversation with Tim Galbraith.'

Hester glared. 'You mean you saw me there and never said a word?'

'Yes,' he rapped, suddenly furious. 'Seeing you both quite literally tête-à-tête, I went out again pretty damn quick and went home. I've been waiting for you to tell me about it. Instead, you lied—told me you were with David and Tally. I detest lies,' he added vehemently, his eyes flashing green like an angry panther.

'So you were waiting for me to confess,' said Hester, suddenly very much on her dignity. 'Setting a little trap for me, too.'

He leaned forward, his eyes boring into hers. 'You told me Galbraith was history. So why the hell were you lunching with him, Hester?'

'I wasn't.' She shrugged indifferently. 'I was with David and Tally, just as I said. Tim came in at the coffee stage and begged a few words with me on my own. Which is what you saw—Tim Galbraith asking if there was any chance for him. I let him know there wasn't, both in the King's Arms and outside the shop in full view of the town. I gave him a dressing down for spiking my drinks that night and sent him on his way. I didn't tell you because I thought you'd be annoyed. You can check with David, if you like.'

Patrick looked at her in silence, his jaw set, then at last he let out a deep, unsteady breath. 'Hester, I'm sorry. I was so bloody jealous, and then when you didn't mention it I thought—'

'What did you think?' she asked curiously. 'Didn't it occur to you, Mr City Lawyer, that if I was seeing Tim I chose a pretty public place to do it? Not,' she added acidly, 'in some secluded out-of-the-way rendezvous. Like you.'

'If you mean Bredecote Hall, at that stage I was merely trying to find a place unlikely to be swarming with your chums—'

'No, not that. I mean the blonde you were entertaining in some little hideaway on Thursday!'

Patrick stared at her blankly. Then, to her fury, threw back his head and roared with laughter. Hester glared at him, incensed, and got up from the table, pushing her chair away so violently it overturned. Patrick jumped to his feet and caught her resistant, unwilling body in his arms.

'Hester, it was *Lily*,' he gasped, and shook her slightly. 'Lily Deakin.'

Hester calmed down a little, her eyes staring up into his suspiciously. 'Is that the truth?'

'I don't lie,' he said flatly, the laughter gone.

'So why didn't you tell me about it?' she demanded.

Patrick released her slowly, putting her away from him a little. 'I came into town to tell you about it. But I saw you with Galbraith.'

'And that's why you've been so abstracted all evening. You were waiting for my confession.'

'Yes. Wasn't it Robert Louis Stevenson who said "the cruellest lies are often told in silence"?' He touched a hand to her cheek and winced as she flinched away from his touch. 'But you weren't lying, silently or otherwise, and neither was I. But due to that bastard Galbraith we've spent a miserable evening—two days on my part.'

'Why didn't you just ask me outright about Tim?' said Hester dully.

Patrick's mouth twisted. 'I wanted you to tell me without being asked.'

They looked at each other for a long, tense moment.

'I love you, Hester,' he said softly.

Her anger melted. 'I love you, too, Patrick.'

They moved together as though pulled by the same string, and fell into each other's arms—Hester trembling as though they'd pulled back from some abyss as they kissed feverishly to blot out the pain of doubt. It was a long time before Patrick was sufficiently recovered to let her go for a moment.

'Where are you going?' said Hester, unwilling to break physical contact.

'I've got a little treat for you,' he said, and kissed her nose. 'It's in the car.'

He returned a moment later with a carrier bag containing a bulky object. 'Lily,' he said in triumph, 'lent me this. Only we must be very careful with it, and we must take it back when I take you to Avecote to meet her.'

'What is it?' asked Hester eagerly, then her eyes opened wide as Patrick withdrew a photograph album from the bag. She looked up at him in excitement, and he nodded.

'Grace Latimer's. She left it to Lily in her will.'

Reverently they opened the album to look at the first pages, which held sepia-tinted wedding photographs—the smiling, large-eyed bride in white, with a sheaf of lilies and gauzy veil, seated, the bridegroom, proud in his dress uniform, standing erect, beside her, one hand on his sword, the other, possessive, on the back of her chair. More photographs showed ladies with large hats and high-boned collars above heroic, corseted bosoms, partnered by solemn men encased in stiff morning dress, and a gaggle of bridesmaids in flowing dresses, rosebud posies in their hands.

'Lieutenant and Mrs Latimer,' said Hester rather thickly. She cleared her throat. 'Young Grace was a real beauty, wasn't she? He didn't marry her just for her money.'

Patrick slid an arm round her and bent closer. 'According to Lily, she was still beautiful in her eighties.'

The album was only half-full. After the wedding came photographs of the newly-weds at Long Wivutts, taken in a garden in all its original glory. Grace was in a thin summer dress, her hair in a plait, playing with a black retriever—her young husband in mufti, pale flannels and blazer, smiling at the camera. Their happiness was plain to see. There were shots of the couple together, taken on some seaside holiday, then more back at Long Wivutts—including one of a shy, obviously reluctant woman in a starched white apron.

'The original housekeeper,' said Patrick. 'Lily's mother.'

'Not many,' said Hester, disappointed when she came to a blank page. 'Is that the lot?'

'One more,' said Patrick quietly. 'Turn to the back.'

Hester breathed in sharply as she found a solitary photograph on the last page. It showed rows of white gravestones in an immaculate military cemetery; the stone in the foreground was engraved with a regimental badge and the name of Lieutenant W.H. Latimer, 1915. Under the photograph, in Grace's handwriting, was the single word 'Picardy'—terse, stark and self-explanatory for those familiar with the First World War.

'Poor little Grace,' said Hester huskily. She closed the album carefully, then laid it on the cushion beside her and turned blindly into Patrick's waiting arms. 'Such a waste,' she said into his chest.

'Now you can see why I waited to show you the album until we were in private,' he said, holding her tightly.

Hester returned his embrace, then she frowned against his shirt and pulled away to look up at him. 'If you were having lunch with Lily, who was the blonde? Or was that Tim's invention?'

'No.' Patrick grinned widely. 'Though he must have seen her from a distance. Lily isn't growing old gracefully, like Mrs Latimer. She's fighting old age tooth and nail, with thick layers of make-up and a blonde curly wig. I adored her on sight.'

Hester chuckled, feeling limp with relief. ''When can I meet her?'

'Any time you like. I thought you might like to hang onto the album for a while. We'll take it back next weekend some time.' He went on to recount some of Lily's anecdotes, about how Mrs Latimer mourned her young husband in dignified solitude until the armistice in 1918. Then cast off her widow's weeds and came out of retirement. She became a stalwart member of St Hilda's church in Avecote, worked tirelessly to make her garden a showplace, and opened it in summer to the public, giving the proceeds to charity. During the Second World War she organised Dig for Victory campaigns, and turned the garden at Long Wivutts over to vegetables, kept poultry, knitted endlessly for the troops, and took in evacuees from London's East End.

'And how did Lily like that?' said Hester, fascinated.

'Not much at first. But when the children went back to London Lily said it was a job to know who cried most—the evacuees, Mrs Latimer or Lily Deakin.'

'Does Lily know why there's been such a turnover in tenants since Mrs Latimer died?'

Patrick nodded. 'They all thought it was haunted.'

'By Grace?'

'Oddly enough, no. According to Lily—who might be exaggerating, of course—later tenants reported hearing other people in the house. In the plural. She was curious to know if I felt that.'

'Do you?'

'No.' He smiled. 'Like you, I just feel as though I belong there. No ghosts, no bumps in the night. And certainly no appearances by the bewitching Grace Latimer, alas.'

They sat, holding each other for a long time, until Patrick stirred at last, reluctantly.

'It's time I went home.'

Hester nodded, sighing. 'What time are we due at your sister's tomorrow?'

'About one.'

'I hope she likes me,' said Hester soberly.

'Of course she will. And even if she doesn't it

won't make any difference.' Patrick raised her face to his. 'I don't just *like* you—I'm crazy about you.' His eyes narrowed. 'If your mother hadn't liked me would it have made any difference to you?'

'None,' said Hester, getting up. 'But I'm glad she approved this time.'

Patrick jumped up, frowning. 'Didn't your mother like Richard?'

'Oh, yes. She liked him. But she thought he was too old for me.' Hester looked away. 'There were twenty-five years between my father and mother, and, as I told you, he died when I was small. Mother didn't want me to marry someone so much older than myself in case the same thing happened. And of course it did.'

Patrick took her in his arms. 'So my age was a recommendation, if nothing else.'

'Don't be modest, Patrick. My mother adored you on sight!'

'Good. But more important still, Hester—do *you* adore me?'

'Yes,' she said starkly. 'I do.'

Patrick's arms tightened as he bent his head to kiss her. 'Likewise, my darling.'

When Patrick came for her next day Hester was ready and waiting in the amber linen dress. 'Will I do?' she asked anxiously, when Patrick had kissed her.

He held her away, looked her up and down, nodded, then kissed her again. 'Oh, yes, you'll do. And now, I suppose,' he added, laughing, 'I'm covered with lipstick?'

Hester shook her head smugly. 'I didn't put any on.

Waste of time. Now I will,' she said, dodging his outstretched hands.

Ashdown House was a modern house, rather like the Raymonds' home but considerably larger, with a garden to match. Hester was prey to unusual nerves as Patrick helped her out of the Jeep—but almost at once the front door opened and a heavily built man with greying dark hair came, smiling, to meet them, hand outstretched.

'Hello. You're Hester, and I'm Jack Barclay. Glad to know you. Come in, come in.'

Hester liked him, rather amused to see no trace of his blond, elegant sons in this rather formidable man. 'Congratulations on your daughter, Mr Barclay—'

'Jack, please.' He led the way through a square, formal hall, with a familiar gilt-framed mirror in pride of place, into a large drawing room which had obviously been newly decorated. 'Just finished the extension on this place,' he said. 'Sorry about the smell of paint. Lydia can't bear it so we're out on the terrace for lunch.'

Hester followed her host out to a tree-shaded terrace, with a striped canopy providing shelter for several garden chairs. Lydia Barclay, in loose white muslin shirt and pink cotton trousers, rose from one, smiling, and held out her hand.

'Hello, Hester. We meet at last. Thank you for the beautiful flowers.'

'It's very good of you to ask me when your daughter's so new.' Hester handed over a parcel tied with pink ribbons. 'I had fun choosing this, but if it's not right you can change it at the shop in the arcade in town.'

Lydia took it with pleased thanks, reached up to

kiss her brother, then unwrapped the parcel eagerly while Jack enquired about drinks. His wife took out minute dungarees, T-shirt and socks, all in the same flower-scattered pink, and gave Hester an impulsive kiss.

'They're so lovely!' she exclaimed. 'Look, Jack!'

Hester relaxed, and took the chair Patrick drew up for her.

'Give her a mineral water—she doesn't drink, Jack,' he said, grinning. 'Or only once in a blue moon. She's a magistrate, remember.'

Hester could have kicked him, but Lydia leaned over and touched her hand. 'Don't be embarrassed. I wanted you to come round today, specifically, because the twins haven't finished school yet. I thought you might like to meet us in stages.' She shrugged fatalistically. 'Thank God Joanna is one of a kind. I'm too old to run round after another pair of twins.'

'Where is the baby?' asked Hester eagerly.

'She's asleep in Jack's study, behind us.' Lydia waved a hand at the little loudspeaker on the table beside her. 'We'll hear her on this the moment she wakes, but would you mind if we postpone a viewing? I rather hoped to eat my lunch before she wants hers.'

Patrick went off to help his sister bring out bowls of pasta and salad, giving Jack Barclay a moment alone with Hester.

'Sorry about those young devils of mine,' he said bluntly. 'Might as well get it out in the open; I know you were on the bench that day. I was worried as hell about the effect on Lydia. The last couple of months of her pregnancy went hard for her. And, of course, when their case came up I was stuck in the States. Patrick was a rock. I owe him.'

Hester found she liked this straight-talking man. 'If you don't mind, Jack,' she said, equally blunt, 'I'd rather we forgot the whole thing. I keep that side of my life strictly separate.'

'Point taken.' He nodded, approving. 'But aren't you a bit young to be a magistrate?'

'I'm in the required age group, and four years over the lower limit.'

He raised bushy dark eyebrows. 'Are you, by Jove? When Patrick hoisted you out of that Jeep of his just now I thought he was cradle-snatching.'

She laughed delightedly. 'If that's a compliment, thank you.'

'What's he saying?' demanded Patrick, a filled plate in one hand, knife and fork and napkin in the other.

'Nice things.' Hester stared at the plate in surprise. 'Is that for me? Why, thank you, but I could have done this myself.'

'My pleasure, darling.'

Lydia Barclay was obviously deeply fond of her brother, and after a few minutes' general conversation she told Hester frankly that she felt happier now they'd met. 'Patrick was off women for a long time after Alicia—' She stopped, eyeing Hester uneasily.

'It's all right,' said Patrick cheerfully. 'I told her all about Alicia's inexplicable preference for a filthy-rich, handsome Yankee lawyer.'

There was general laughter until Lydia bent her head towards the baby listener. 'My daughter.' She hurried into the house, and a minute later opened the study window and leaned out. 'I'm going to feed Joanna in here. Would you like to keep me company, Hester?'

Hester was out of her seat like a shot, and went inside to find Lydia changing her protesting daughter's nappy. Hester knelt on the floor to look at the tiny, wriggling body and failing hands, and there was an ache somewhere in the region of her midriff as Lydia fastened the last popper on Joanna's daisy-printed bodysuit.

'Up you come, popsie.' Lydia got to her feet with the baby in her arms. 'Would you like to hold her while I get her bottle?'

Hester received the warm little bundle gingerly, smiling down into the tiny pink face. To her surprise a pair of bright blue eyes seemed to be studying her face intently. 'Hello, Joanna Barclay,' she said softly. 'You're a very beautiful girl.'

'So are you,' said Patrick from the doorway, and Hester looked up to find him watching her in a way which turned her heart over.

'You must have the magic touch, Hester,' said Lydia, brushing past him with the baby's milk. 'She's usually raising the roof at this stage.'

Hester handed the baby over reluctantly, then sat down to watch as Joanna began drinking her milk.

'Anything I can fetch you ladies?' asked Patrick.

'Could you ask Jack to make us some tea?' said his sister. 'Unless you'd prefer coffee, Hester?'

'She likes tea better,' said Patrick, and strolled off to do his sister's bidding.

'Do you love him?' asked Lydia, without warning.

Hester blinked. 'Yes, I do,' she said, after a pause. 'I've only known him a short time, so I suppose it seems very sudden to you.'

'Not in the least.' Lydia removed the teat from her daughter's mouth, put the bottle down on her husband's desk and held the baby up against her shoulder, patting the tiny back. 'The minute I saw Jack I knew I'd marry him. And Patrick's a lot prettier than Jack.'

Hester laughed involuntarily. 'You wouldn't be prejudiced in your brother's favour, by any chance?'

'Of course I am. But I'm not blind to his faults, either.'

'So he does have some?' asked Hester teasingly.

'Of course he does. But his good points far outweigh the not-so-good.' Joanna gave an explosive burp, and Lydia showered her daughter with praise and resumed feeding her. When the milk was all gone Lydia got up, handed Hester a muslin square to drape over her shoulder and gave her the baby. 'Perhaps you'd like to burp her for me while I wash her bottle and see what's happened to our tea.'

Hester was quite overcome with the pleasure she felt in holding the warm little body against her shoulder, her cheek against the downy fair head. She patted gently, as she'd seen Lydia doing, and after a while got another little explosion as her reward. She laughed delightedly, told Joanna she was a clever girl, then walked up and down the small room, patting gently until she realised, not without pride, that the baby was asleep.

'Oh, well done,' said Lydia, coming back. 'I'll put her down for a while, and Jack and Patrick can listen for her while I show you what we've been doing with the house.'

The Barclays had spent their time since moving into Ashdown House in enlarging it. Lydia and the house had grown together, the former said, laughing, as she took Hester through the rooms. A study had been needed for Jack, and separate rooms for the first time for Dominic and Giles. The sitting room had been extended, and the terrace paved with local stone slabs. The Barclays had moved several times previously, as Jack Barclay gained regular promotion until his present status as vice-president of a well-known electronics company.

'We bought this place for Jack's retirement,' said Lydia as they came to rest in the drawing room. 'He'll keep a flat in town and come home on weekends and so on until then.'

Hester's attention was caught by various photographs in silver frames on a writing desk. She smiled at the brand new study of baby Joanna, with her parents' wedding portrait behind it, and a brother on either side. Hester's eyes narrowed. In one photograph Dominic—or Giles—looked very much the same as on his appearance in court. In the other one the boy was dressed in an identical white shirt, but his striped tie was slightly askew and his hair needed cutting.

'You're looking at my terrible two,' said Lydia, at Hester's elbow. 'Giles arrived half an hour before his brother—so different from Dominic in some ways, yet in others the two of them function like one person.'

When they returned to join the men, Hester joined in the general conversation for a while, then rose. 'It's time we went, Lydia. You look tired.'

'I am a bit. I'll just feed Joanna again, then Jack can entertain her while I have a nap.' Lydia smiled ruefully. 'At my age I need a nap anyway, baby or not.'

Hester went in to see the baby, and, since the little bundle was stirring, asked permission to pick Joanna up and have another cuddle before she left. She laid her cheek to the damp, satiny warmth of the baby's, then relinquished Joanna to her mother, promising to come and visit again soon.

On the short drive back to the cottage Hester said very little, and yawned a little to justify her silence. Patrick followed her into the cottage, and sat down with the air of a man very much in possession, and, where it had thrilled her before, Hester now resented it.

'Patrick,' she began, but he held up his arms.

'Come and kiss me,' he interrupted, then eyed her searchingly. 'Ah. You don't want to. What's the matter, Hester?'

'On my tour of Ashdown House I saw some photographs of the twins.'

Patrick's eyes narrowed. 'As well you might. Lydia's quite expert with a camera.'

'These were formal photographs. In the drawing room on the writing desk.'

He frowned. 'I don't think I've seen those. But that room's only just been completed. Lydia probably rushed to put them there today, to show them to you.' He got up and took her hand. 'Something's obviously wrong.'

'If I ask you something,' she said tonelessly, 'will you tell me the truth?'

'You know damn well I will,' he said, astonished. 'So, what's bothering you?'

'I think we'd better sit down, Patrick.' Hester sat in a chair and waved Patrick to the sofa. 'As you know,' she went on, 'I never discuss court cases. But in this instance I must. Did you prepare the twins for their day in court—the day I first saw you?'

'I know perfectly well which day you mean,' he

said brusquely. He looked across at her, his eyes resigned and oddly hard. 'And the answer's no. I gather that in these photographs you saw they looked different?'

'Very.' Her lips tightened. 'But before they went to court they had their hair cut to match, and on the day wore their school uniform to complete the picture.'

'Right.'

'But it *was* Dominic who drove the car, wasn't it?'

'Yes.'

'And you knew this.'

He put out a hand in appeal. 'Hester, let me explain—'

'Patrick,' she broke in relentlessly, 'did you know it or not?'

He looked at her for a long, tense interval, then shrugged, his face drained of expression. 'Guilty as charged.'

Silence settled over the room like a thick, smothering blanket.

Integrity, she thought bitterly. The man who loathes lies in any shape or form.

At last Patrick got to his feet. 'You've got it wrong, Hester.'

'I don't think so.' She looked at him coldly. 'You know, better than anyone, that Dominic could have got a custodial sentence because he was already disqualified from driving. Six months in prison, to be precise.'

'Yes, of course I knew.'

It was silly to feel so stunned. Patrick was only confirming what she'd known, in her heart of hearts, all along. Ever since the day in court. But at that time

Hester Conway, JP, had not been head over heels in love with Patrick Hazard and preparing to spend the rest of her life with him. And, said a nagging voice in her head, if he could bend the law to his purpose in this instance, could he be trusted in other ways in the future? Yes, of course, said her heart. Who knows? said her mind.

'Were you ever going to tell me?' asked Hester at last.

He looked her in the eye. 'To be honest, no. Unless absolutely necessary. Does it make such a difference?'

'I'd be lying if I said it didn't. And you detest lies,' she reminded him. 'Yet in a way you have been lying to me on this issue.'

'I have not, Hester,' he retorted coldly. 'The subject never came up.'

'Weren't you the one who said the cruellest lies are told in silence?'

Patrick shrugged wearily. 'The truth wasn't mine to tell. It's as simple as that. Perhaps if you weren't a magistrate I might have told you, so that nothing was secret between us. But I thought it would be difficult for you to deal with. And I'm right. Aren't I?' he added with sudden vehemence.

'Yes,' said Hester without emotion. 'You are.'

Patrick reached down and took her hand to pull her up, but when he would have taken her in his arms she stepped back and his hands fell. He looked at her with eyes like slivers of green ice. 'Are you actually allowing this to come between us, Hester?'

She hugged her arms across her chest, feeling cold. 'Illogical, I know, but it came as a blow. It shouldn't have, because deep down I've known all along. I just didn't expect to find confirmation of it so hard.'

'Are you saying that it's over between us because of this?' he said incredulously.

Hester swallowed. 'No. Not over. I just think we should slow things down a bit; take time to get to know each other better.'

Patrick's eyes glittered in the sudden pallor of his face. 'So, Madam Justice, because my nephew got off scot-free you're going to make *me* suffer instead?'

'Certainly not!' she said angrily.

'No? But I am to take myself off home and wait tamely until you've had time to think things over and decide whether I'm to be trusted.' He smiled sardonically. 'Perhaps Richard might have been indulgent with you, but I warn you now, Hester—I'm not the indulgent type. Neither am I cut out to be docile, waiting patiently to see what scraps of your company you care to dole out—'

'That's not fair,' she said hotly. 'I just want more time to adjust to the idea.'

'The idea of sharing your life with me?'

'Yes,' she said evenly. 'It's a big step. It's only sensible to get to know each other better before we get married—'

'Married?' Patrick gave her a slow, scathing smile which turned her blood cold. 'Who said anything about marriage, Hester?'

A wave of colour flooded her face then receded again. Hester's chin lifted proudly as she forced herself to meet his eyes head-on. 'How very embarrassing. No point in lying—you don't like that—so I admit I took it for granted. Probably because I was married before. My mistake.' She went to the door and opened it. 'If you don't mind, I'd appreciate some time alone now.'

Patrick stood close beside her, looking down into her composed face. 'Are you saying it's a wedding ring or nothing?'

'I already have a wedding ring. But if you mean I'm no longer available for sessions in your bed, yes.' She gave him a tight little smile. 'A lady magistrate is expected to keep to the rules. I'm not sure what the actual rules are on co-habiting, because it's never come up. But since I am a Justice of the Peace my own personal code doesn't include shacking up with a lover.'

'Beautifully put, Hester,' he said with deep distaste. 'After that there doesn't seem anything left to say. Except goodbye.'

CHAPTER ELEVEN

HESTER watched him stride down the path to the gate, then shut her door and raced upstairs. She stripped off her clothes and ran the shower as hot as she could bear it, then so cold that her teeth were chattering as she towelled herself dry. But it was no use as a remedy. She still burned with humiliation. How could she have been such a *fool*? She shivered with self-disgust. Idiot. Imbecile. Taking marriage for granted when all Patrick wanted was sex! She would never forget the scathing look on his face. Never.

To channel off her fury Hester went out into the garden and began mowing the lawn. Afterwards she edged and hoed and weeded, then went on to snip off all the dead blooms, forced to stop at last before she deflowered her entire garden. But none of it salved the wound Patrick had inflicted. She still felt raw and bleeding inside, and in the end she got out Richard's petrol-driven hedge-cutter. David always trimmed her hedges, but today it was the kind of exhausting job she badly needed.

Hester set to with a will, though at first she had difficulty in yanking the engine into motion. Once started she didn't dare stop, and proceeded down the inner privet hedge with determination. Like Sherman through Georgia, she thought with grim satisfaction. But Hester, several inches shorter than David, lacked his reach. At last she stretched too far, overbalanced, and screamed as the saw teeth of the blade ripped into her thigh before she could manage to fling the hedge-cutter away.

Panting, covered in perspiration already turning cold with shock, blood streaming down her bare leg, Hester switched off the hedge-cutter with shaking fingers and limped into the house. With a wet tea-towel clamped against her thigh she rang David, and shortly afterwards—by which time she was feeling very peculiar indeed—David and Tally arrived to rush her off to the medical centre, where they'd asked Dr Meadows to meet them.

'Lucky I'm an old-fashioned, hands-on type of medico,' said her fellow magistrate, after he'd cleansed and injected and got to work with needle and sutures in the minor ops room. 'By rights you should have gone off to Casualty.'

'Sorry.' Hester had managed to get through life up to this point without stitches in any part of her person, and had not enjoyed her new experience.

'What the hell were you doing, cutting hedges?' demanded a green-faced David wrathfully. 'It's not even time yet, and in any case you know I'll do it for you!'

'Stop shouting at her,' said Tally, glaring at him, and handed Hester a glass of water. 'Drink this, love.'

'You'll have to keep off that leg for a while,' warned Dr Meadows, packing his bag. 'Make her take a holiday, David. She looks tired. I'll inform John Brigham. Someone else can sit in for you on Friday in court, Hester.'

'No one looks their best under these circumstances,' protested a much-tried Hester. 'And I'll go mad on my own doing nothing.'

'Don't worry—you're coming home with us,' said Tally.

'So don't argue,' ordered David.

Hester found she was not averse to the idea. It would be comforting to be coddled and fussed over for a change.

After a couple of days of it, however, she felt physically better, but so depressed otherwise that it was exhausting to hide it. When Robert heard of her accident he came to visit and listened with sympathy when Hester told him her relationship with Patrick was over.

'Are you sure?' he asked gently.

'Afraid so.' Hester sighed and shifted her bruised, wounded leg.

'Pity.' He said no more. But later that night Tally picked up the phone after dinner, then handed it to Hester.

'For you.'

Hester almost snatched it in her eagerness, hard put to it to hide her disappointment when she heard her mother's voice. Robert had rung Celia Lucas with the news, and she was hopping mad because her daughter had kept quiet about her accident.

'I didn't want to worry you, Mother,' said Hester wearily.

'Idiot child. Get David to put you on the train and I'll pick you up in Leamington. Time you came home for a while.'

Hester spent two weeks in Warwick, in the small cottage with a view across the river to the ancient, impressive castle. Once Celia learned that Patrick was history she asked why, listened to the reason, saw that

Hester found the subject painful and never mentioned it again. It was a healing process, Hester found, to sleep in her old room, with its spectacular view, to limp along the riverbank with Paris and Aggie when her leg was better, and eventually to hold court when friends came to visit.

Glad of the respite, but more than ready to return to her job and the routine of her days in Chastlecombe, Hester was glad when her mother offered to drive her back.

'I'll just stay the night and settle you in, but I must get back for Paris and Aggie. They hate going to kennels.'

'Actually they love it, Mother,' said Hester, amused. 'It's you who hates it.'

Hester's first instinct when she unlocked her front door was to check her messages, but there weren't any—from Patrick or anyone else. The machine wasn't working.

'I'll just pop upstairs to the other phone to ring Tally. There's something the matter with this one.'

'Go carefully,' said Celia sharply. 'Mind that leg.'

Hester went upstairs, dumped her suitcase on the bed, then rang Tally to say she was back, and to learn there had been a bad storm the day after she'd left for Warwick.

'My answer machine was probably struck by lightning,' she told Celia when she went downstairs. 'I can't even claim that on insurance—act of God, or something.'

'Well, get another one at once. I like to leave a message when I don't get you.' Celia eyed her daughter's brown face. 'At least you've managed to get a nice brown glow by sitting in the garden at home so much. You never sit in this one.'

'No. I'm too busy working in it.' Hester gazed through the window despondently. 'I left it immaculate—and now look at it!'

After Celia left Hester felt lonely. No one knew she was back, other than the Conways, and Tally was helping out in the shop in her place. But as yet she didn't feel like getting back to work. Her leg was still painful; the thought of standing around on it held no appeal at all. But at least this week she could do her stint in court. And she could do some pruning and dead-heading—even a bit of weeding, if she took care. Machinery of any kind she would leave for a while.

And of Patrick she refused to think at all. During the time since their last meeting the burning humiliation had been replaced by an odd blankness, an absence of feeling of any kind other than the persistent throbbing as her wound healed.

Unable to kneel to do her weeding, Hester was attacking her borders with a hoe next day when she found she had company. She was wearing the khaki shorts and yellow vest, a baseball cap low over her eyes to keep out sun and sweat, when she was astonished to find two familiar young men advancing up her path.

'Is Mrs Conway in?' said one of them, and Hester stripped off her gardening gloves and the cap, letting her hair loose.

'Yes, I am. Good morning.'

Two identical faces stared at her in shock.

'Sorry, Mrs Conway,' said one of them hurriedly. 'We didn't recognise you. Do you remember us?'

Was she ever likely to forget?

'Yes, indeed.' Hester looked from one to the other. They both wore jeans. One of them had an immaculate blue T-shirt, the other boy's was grey and frankly grubby. One head of blond hair was long but well cut, the other shaggy and obviously untrimmed for some time. 'You're Dominic?' she said to the immaculate one.

'No, I'm Giles.' The boys looked at each other, then Giles looked at Hester in appeal. 'Mrs Conway, could we talk to you for a minute, please?'

'Of course.' Wildly curious, Hester led the way into the house. 'Would you like some coffee, or a drink?'

'Coffee would be great,' said Dominic, his eyes falling to the eye-catching scar on Hester's bare brown thigh. 'Crikey, Mrs Conway—how did you do that?'

'Hedge-cutter,' she said briefly, and went to fill the kettle.

When they were all seated, mugs in hand, Hester eyed them expectantly.

'So, why did you want to talk to me?'

'My mother says you and Patrick were friends. But now you're not, and we're to blame,' blurted Dominic.

'So we thought we'd come and explain things,' said Giles, colouring.

'How nice of you,' said Hester, touched.

The boys exchanged one of their looks, then Dominic squared his shoulders.

'I'm to blame. In the beginning, I mean. I'm the one who got disqualified—had some beer at a party and thought I was under the limit, but I wasn't. I got caught, which serves me right.'

'Then the night the policewoman saw him driving the car, I was away, visiting a girlfriend, and Mother was taken ill,' Giles went on. 'Dad was away, and Patrick was in London. Mum thought she was losing the baby, so Dominic drove her to the hospital.'

His brother nodded glumly. 'Afterwards Patrick played hell, said we should have called a taxi, but at the time both Mum and I were in a panic so I took a chance. But the policewoman spotted me. Sod's law. Sorry!' he added, flushing.

'I see. So Patrick told you to get your hair cut and swap identities, with Giles playing the defendant and Dominic in the witness box,' said Hester.

'Good lord, no, Mrs Conway. I mean, that's what we did, but Patrick didn't tell us to. We thought it up ourselves. Ma was in such a state about me, we had to do something. I was afraid I'd get six months in the slammer, and we thought that would make her lose the baby, even that she might—might die.' Dominic swallowed hard. 'So we hatched up the plan without telling anyone. But the only lies we told were our names,' he added, and looked at her uneasily.

'So in the witness box, when you were asked if you were driving, you were able to say with complete truth that you were,' said Hester slowly.

The boys nodded, then gulped down their coffee in unison.

'Patrick played hell with us afterwards when he found out what we'd done,' said Giles glumly. 'You probably saw him giving us a going over in the King's Arms.'

'Good job Dad was in America,' said Dominic with

feeling. 'He goes up like a rocket when we upset Mother, believe me.'

'I've met him—I do believe you,' said Hester, still trying to take it in.

'Anyway, Mrs Conway, the only lies we told were our names. But Patrick didn't know what we were up to until he saw Dominic in the witness box. But we actually said the truth—only everyone thought I was Dominic, and vice versa.' Giles looked at Hester squarely. 'Do you have to report this?'

'In my capacity as a magistrate, you mean?' Hester thought about it. 'I would have to take instruction on that. Not that I will.' She looked at them sternly. 'For your mother's sake I'm going to forget we ever had this conversation.'

They grinned widely in relief, and jumped up. 'Thank you, Mrs Conway,' said Dominic fervently, then hesitated. 'Does it make a difference? With you and Patrick?'

For a variety of reasons Hester doubted it very much. She smiled noncommittally as she limped down the path with them. 'By the way, how did your exams go?'

'Pretty well, actually,' said Giles. 'With a bit of luck we're probably both off to Cambridge in the autumn.'

'Congratulations. What are you reading?'

'Law!' they chorused, grinning.

Hester shook her head, laughing. 'Good. Stick to the right side of it in future. Give my love to your mother and baby sister—I've been away; I only got back yesterday.'

'I know—we've been round before a couple of times. Were you on holiday?' asked Giles.

She pointed at the scar. 'I went home to my mother to get over this.'

'Ma said would you fancy coming round to supper tomorrow evening?' asked Dominic. 'She said she wouldn't take offence if you didn't in the circumstances. Because of us, I mean.'

'Tell her I'd love to,' said Hester. 'As long as I can cuddle Joanna for a while.'

'Feel free,' said Giles with feeling. 'Boy, can she raise the roof sometimes!'

'Is it odd, having a baby sister at your age?' said Hester curiously.

They grinned.

'Odd,' said Dominic. 'But nice, too. She's cute— and we're both jolly glad she arrived safely. We were worried sick about Ma beforehand.'

Hester waved them off, feeling sightly better than at any time since her farewell from Patrick. But only slightly. It was a relief to find he hadn't been as unprincipled as she'd thought. But his scorn on the subject of marriage still burned, indelible, like a brand on her heart.

David and Tally came round in the evening to bring Hester up to date on the local news and report on affairs at Conway's.

'That new consignment of china came in, also the bedroom furniture you ordered,' said David, and eyed her warily. 'We delivered the furniture out to Long Wivutts ten days ago, by the way.'

'Good. I trust the owner was satisfied with everything?' said Hester lightly.

'Talking of which,' said Tally, taking a newspaper out of her bag, 'we thought you might like to see this.'

Hester looked at the centre page of the local weekly newspaper, her heart giving a sick thump as she saw Patrick's photograph—Patrick, in city-suited elegance, hair gleaming, acknowledging the toasts of a group of smiling people.

Patrick Hazard, thirty-six, attractive lawyer turned author, has recently taken possession of Long Wivutts, a charming house outside Avecote. He is photographed here at the launch of his book, *A Law Unto Himself*. The handsome, unmarried author's first venture into fiction is a thriller with a courtroom background, tipped to be a runaway bestseller.

'Cathy Porter's journalistic style tends to the florid,' said Hester dryly, putting the paper down. 'I must have words with her next time I beat her at tennis.'

'Which won't be for a while yet,' said David. 'How's the leg?'

'Practically healed. I went round to Dr Meadows this afternoon.' Hester pulled a face. 'He pronounced me fit, gave me a lecture about care with garden machinery and told me I was very lucky to have got off so lightly.'

Tally shuddered. 'You could have hit an artery.' She hesitated. 'I suppose you haven't heard from Patrick?'

'No. Nor do I expect to.' Hester smiled. 'But thanks for showing me the article. It puts things in perspective.'

'How?' demanded David.

'He's at home in that kind of milieu,' she explained, pointing to the picture. 'I'm strictly a small-town girl.'

'What difference does that make?'

'I belong here. And, although he's bought a house in our fashionable Cotswolds, Patrick doesn't.'

'I thought you seemed so right together,' said Tally forlornly.

'Not really. But don't look so sad. There's no harm done.'

Platitudes, thought Hester grimly when they'd gone, were all very well. But in this instance weren't even true. The harm came in having ever set eyes on Patrick in the first place.

Hester woke next morning to a sudden realisation that Lydia Barclay might well invite Patrick round to supper without telling him about the extra guest. And as the day wore on Hester found she just couldn't face the thought of it. She would have to meet Patrick some time, of course. But not this way. She shuddered at the thought, able to picture it all too plainly— Patrick icily polite, and the entire evening in painful contrast to the previous visit to the Barclays'. At last she rang Lydia to lie about a sudden cold in the head, and to say with perfect truth that she was sorry she couldn't make it. Lydia, very plainly, was disappointed, and made Hester promise to let her know the moment she was better.

Afterwards the chilly wet day dragged interminably, until by early evening Hester decided she might as well be miserable in bed as anywhere else. She carried her portable television set up to her bedroom, got undressed and settled down to watch a tear-jerking TV movie from the comfort of her bed.

The film was heart-rending, with a cute little moppet crying for the mother her father refused to let her see. Dramatic music came in lush waves and Hester, her resistance lower than usual, found herself sniffing hard. She reached for a box of tissues and scrubbed at her streaming eyes, telling herself it was only a film. But it was no use. By the time the credits rolled on the final scene, with all three of them reunited to live happily ever after, Hester was a mess. She reached out a hand for a glass of water, then shot upright in bed in terror as her door flew open and Patrick erupted into the room.

'What happened?' he said roughly. 'You didn't answer when I knocked on your door, so I went over to David. He gave me a key—' He broke off, staring at her. 'You look terrible. Why are you crying?'

'I'm not crying,' snapped Hester, tugging the quilt under her chin. 'And what if I am? It's none of your business. Nor,' she added, warming to the theme, 'do I quite see what you're doing in my house.'

'I was worried when you didn't come to Lydia's. She said you were ill.' He advanced to the side of the bed and stood there, arms folded. 'Is that the truth?' His eyes narrowed suddenly, and he bent to put a finger under her chin.

Hester dodged away angrily, wanting to murder him. 'Would you please go away.' If and when she met Patrick again she'd planned to look so gorgeous he would be bowled over at the sight of her. Instead her hair was all over the place, her eyes were red from crying and she was tastefully attired in a pair of ancient striped pyjamas.

His jaw tightened as he stepped back. 'You've obviously got a temperature; I'd better call the doctor.'

'Certainly not. There's nothing the matter with me,' she said irritably.

'You told Lydia you had a cold,' he pointed out.

She glared at him. 'I lied.'

'Why? To avoid running into me, by any chance?'

'Precisely.'

'Which doesn't explain why you've obviously been crying your eyes out.' To Hester's dismay he drew up a chair to the bed with the air of a man settling down to a long discussion.

As always, to Hester, he looked wonderful, in a pale linen suit, creased enough to look exactly right, and a white shirt open at the collar. He was a sight for sore eyes, which hers most certainly were. And she wished he'd take his elegant person off and leave her alone. 'Would you mind going now, please?' she asked with dignity.

'Yes, I would,' he said flatly. 'Which reminds me—I'd better ring David and tell him you're not lying unconscious on the floor.'

'I'll do that—'

'I promised him *I* would.' He reached for the receiver from her bedside table.

She clenched her teeth and slid further under the covers, listening while Patrick reassured Tally, telling her not to worry and that he would make sure Hester was all right before he went home.

'*If* I go home,' he added, eyeing the list of names on the phone.

She glared at him. 'What do you mean *if*? And do feel free to use my phone as much as you like, of course. Who are you ringing now?'

'Your doctor.'

'I don't *need* a doctor. I saw one this afternoon.'

'Why?' he said sharply.

'To check on my leg. I had a bit of an accident with the hedge-cutter.'

'So I heard. But not until tonight, from the twins,' he added bitterly. 'No one saw fit to tell *me*, of course—something I pointed out to David. When I rang the shop to speak to you last week one of your assistants told me you were away on holiday.'

'I went to stay with my mother,' she muttered, and shifted uneasily in the bed.

'What's the matter—do you feel sick?' he demanded, jumping up.

'No!' Hester blushed like a schoolgirl. 'I just need to go to the bathroom.'

Patrick handed her the white towelling robe, and in embarrassed silence Hester wrapped it round herself and went from the room with as much dignity as she could muster. She took advantage of her time in the bathroom to splash some cold water on her eyes, brushed out her hair and went back to the bedroom to find Patrick had tidied it and stacked the pillows neatly.

'To return to my earlier question—why didn't you open the door?' he said as she slid hastily into bed.

'I didn't hear you knocking. I was watching a very sad TV movie with the volume up. Lots of melodramatic music. Which is why I was crying. It was a four-hankie tear-jerker.' She smiled at him frostily. 'Did you think I was crying over you, by any chance?'

'You should have been,' he said malevolently, and went to the door. 'I'll make you some tea.'

Hester opened her mouth to tell him to go away, that she didn't want any tea, then closed it again—

because she did want tea, and she wanted him to stay. So much that she was furious with herself.

Patrick returned in a remarkably short time, minus the linen jacket, carrying a tea-tray laid for two. He filled a beaker and handed it to Hester. She thanked him politely, telling him there was beer in the refrigerator if he would like some.

'I'd rather share your tea, thanks.' He filled a second mug and sat down again in the small basket chair, his long legs stretched out in front of him.

Hester sipped cautiously. The tea tasted like nectar. She looked at him levelly. 'You don't have to stay, now you know there's nothing wrong with me.'

'Give me time to drink the tea, at least.' His eyes clashed with hers, and she found herself forced to look away.

'Of course. How's Joanna?'

For a short interval they talked awkwardly, in stilted words so unlike their previous communion that Hester wanted to cry again. She asked him politely about the book launch and he replied in kind, adding that the press's opinion of the book's chances was probably a lot too optimistic.

Patrick stared down into his tea. 'I could let you have a copy, if you like.'

'Oh, I would,' she said instantly. 'Very much.'

'I'll bring one over.' He breathed in impatiently and looked up. 'For God's sake, let's stop fencing, Hester. I gather Giles and Dominic paid you a visit yesterday?'

'Yes. They gave me the authorised version of what happened that day in court.'

'Did their confession dispose you more kindly towards me?'

She shrugged. 'Somewhat, yes. I was relieved to find you weren't quite as devious as I'd thought.'

'Duped—not devious,' he said harshly. 'I didn't realise they'd done a swap until it dawned on me that it was Giles in the dock.'

'So I gather,' she said politely.

Patrick's jaw tightened. 'And since we're actually face to face at last I've finally got the opportunity to grovel.'

'Grovel? You?' She smiled incredulously.

'Yes,' he said harshly. 'I hurt you deliberately, and I'm not proud of it. But, hell, Hester—you cut me to the heart when you condemned me out of hand, said you needed time to consider. So I cut back. In the cruellest way I could. On the way home I almost turned back several times, bitterly regretting what I'd said. Instead I rang you the moment I got through the door, desperate to explain that I hadn't meant a word of it, that I'd taken it for granted from the first that we'd marry, but all I got was your machine. And that particular message was a bloody difficult one to leave to a machine, believe me.'

She stared at him, her heart thumping, hardly able to believe her ears. 'I slashed my thigh with the hedge-cutter after you left,' she said unsteadily. 'In the uproar no one thought to check my messages.'

He thrust a hand through his hair, shaking his head in disbelief. 'And because of that I've spent the most bloody awful period of my entire life. I rang David, but he was out—'

'Taking me to be stitched up.'

'I wish to God I'd known! Then I had a call from my agent first thing next morning and had to take off for London for the launch. When I got back I rang

David, but he was deliberately vague about where you were and how long you'd be.'

Hester nodded. 'He was acting on instructions. Not,' she added acidly, 'that I expected you to make enquiries.'

'So it seems.' Patrick gave her a fiery look. 'So all I could do was wait. In vain, as it turned out. I didn't know what had actually happened until the twins said you were home, and mentioned the scar on your leg.' He frowned. 'If it's your thigh, how did they come to see it?'

'Shorts,' she said succinctly, feeling better by the minute.

'I didn't come round straight away, as I wanted to, because I thought you might shut the door in my face. So I left it until tonight, when I expected to see you at Lydia's. It seemed unlikely you'd walk out of Ashdown House the moment you set eyes on me. But you didn't come.'

'No. It's been rather hard to forget your parting shot.'

Patrick looked her in the eye. 'We hurt each other, didn't we?' He smiled a little. 'Which is reassuring in one way.'

Hester raised an eyebrow. 'How, exactly?'

He smiled, something in his eyes making her pulse accelerate. 'You know very well, Hester—you only hurt the one you love. And I do love you, Hester. So much I'll take myself off and never bother you again if that's what you really want.'

Her eyes narrowed. 'Would you really do that?'

Patrick hesitated, then he got up and advanced towards the bed, shaking his head. 'No, blast it, I wouldn't. No point in making promises I can't keep.'

He sat down on the edge of the bed. 'Tell me you'll marry me, for God's sake, Hester.' He seized her in his arms and kissed her hungrily, and Hester melted against him, responding so wholeheartedly that Patrick gave a smothered sound and crushed her close.

'Answer me!' he said raggedly, shaking her.

'Can't you recognise a yes?' she gasped, and smiled at him so incandescently that he buried his face against her hair in relief.

'I've got a confession,' he muttered indistinctly.

Hester drew away, eyes narrowed. 'What is it?'

'Before I went out tonight I rang your mother to ask her blessing, and I told David and Tally, too, when I barged in there just now, so you'll have to marry me now.' His arms tightened. 'I would have sent a notice to the local paper as the most effective way, but I need your confirmation for that. So—forgive me, darling—I did the next best thing.'

Hester's eyes widened. 'Tell me the worst.'

'I rang Dan Raymond, on some pretext about the house, and while I was at it mentioned our forthcoming nuptials. Very casually, of course, but Mrs Raymond will probably be out on the town as we speak, spreading the news.' He grinned, the glittering triumph in his eyes so infectious she began to laugh.

'What happens if I deny it?'

'I'll sue you for breach of promise—I'm a lawyer, remember!'

Hester snorted inelegantly. 'A law unto yourself, more like it.'

'That's more or less the title of my book.'

'I know.'

Patrick sat on the edge of the bed and took her hand. 'I love you so much, Hester.'

'Even the way I look now?'

'Especially the way you look now.' He leaned forward and kissed her very gently on the mouth. 'Now show me this scar.'

Hester pushed back the covers and rolled up her pyjama leg. The colour drained from Patrick's face as he stared down at the jagged tear.

'It's healing very well,' she said, and bit her lip. 'It's obviously making you sick to look at it.' She tugged at the quilt, but Patrick stayed her hand and bent his head until his lips touched her skin alongside the scar, then he straightened and pulled her into his arms in a rib-cracking embrace.

'You could have killed yourself,' he said hoarsely. 'Promise me you'll never do anything like that again!'

'I won't, I won't,' she promised, suddenly giddy with happiness. 'Wilf can do the hedges at Long Wivutts.'

Six weeks later—the time it took for her to walk without limping—Hester Conway married Patrick Hazard in a simple civil ceremony very different from the service in St Mary's Church in Warwick, where she'd married Richard.

This time it seemed only sensible to marry in Chastlecombe. At the bride's request there was no formal morning dress for the men, much to the relief of the twins, who nevertheless caused havoc among some young female cousins of Hester. After the ceremony, and the usual photographs, a fair proportion of the inhabitants of Chastlecombe gathered to wish Hester and Patrick happiness at an informal party in the garden at Long Wivutts. Even Tim Galbraith managed to look pleased when he whispered in Hester's ear before going off to mingle with the other guests.

'What did he say?' demanded Patrick.

'He was just telling me that as an appropriate wedding present he's giving us some Judas trees.' Hester smiled up at him radiantly under the brim of her large bronze straw hat, the apricot chiffon of her dress furling about her gently in the breeze, and Patrick bent towards her involuntarily.

'Now, now,' said Annie Raymond, striking as ever in jade-green. 'Keep that for later. Congratulations, my dears!'

After all the hugging and kissing Hester and Patrick wandered hand in hand through their guests, stopping to talk to every group until they reached the Barclays, where Hester detached baby Joanna from her mother.

'My turn,' she said firmly.

'Watch it, Hester,' warned Giles. 'She overflows now and then.'

'I don't mind,' said Hester, laughing, and went on with her tour with Patrick—Joanna in her arms, Lydia watching happily as they bore her daughter away.

It was late by the time the last guest had gone, and Wilf and his wife and various other members of their family—including the redoubtable Lily Deakin—had cleared away the last vestiges of the wedding feast.

'Alone at last,' said Patrick thankfully as Hester subsided on one of the new sofas. 'Mrs Wilf has left us some supper, and I've concocted some Pimm's to celebrate our first night at Long Wivutts as man and wife. It's been a long time,' he added, with feeling.

During the six weeks of their official engagement Patrick had insisted on conducting a very proper, con-

ventional courtship, more of the type Grace Latimer
had once experienced than the usual present-
day arrangement.

'It's a sort of penance on my part for hurting you
so badly,' Patrick had explained. 'Will you miss making love with me?'

'Yes,' Hester had said simply.

'Then in that case it's a penance for you, too, for
hurting me,' he'd informed her promptly.

Now, the waiting over, Hester had no wish to speed
the day. She wanted to catch every moment and hold
it before it slipped away for ever. They sat close
together on the sofa, watching the moon rise over the
garden as they ate their supper, and talked over the
day and how happy it had been.

'And just in case you're wondering,' said Hester,
'I was not haunted by memories of last time.'

'I'm glad. I wondered, but it seemed a bit tactless
to ask.'

'I was happy then,' she said thoughtfully, 'but this
is different.' She turned to look into the intent green
eyes, and touched a hand to Patrick's cheek. 'Then I
was a bride. Tonight I'm a wife. One who loves you
in every way possible.'

Patrick took in a deep, unsteady breath and kissed
her hands. 'Then come upstairs and let me show you
how much I love you.'

It was later that night, when the moonlight was bright
in their room, that Patrick said something which made
Hester's happiness complete.

'You know, darling,' he said casually, 'I've worked
out the secret of Long Wivutts—why we feel so much

at home here, even why the other tenants thought it was haunted.'

'I think I have, too,' said Hester. 'Since Grace left it Long Wivutts has been haunted by the future, not the past.'

'You knew!' Patrick turned her to face him and looked deep in her eyes. 'That's it, exactly. It was forecasting the life you and I will live here with our children.'

Hester tensed. 'What if I can't, Patrick? It never happened with Richard.'

'It will with me,' he assured her with supreme confidence. 'As surely as I'll love you more and more with every passing day.'

And, to Hester's joy, before the year was out Patrick was proved right. On both counts.

MILLS & BOON®

Next Month's Romances

♡

Each month you can choose from a wide variety of romance novels from Mills & Boon. Below are the new titles to look out for next month from the Presents™ and Enchanted™ series.

Presents™

A NANNY FOR CHRISTMAS	Sara Craven
A FORBIDDEN DESIRE	Robyn Donald
THE WINTER BRIDE	Lynne Graham
THE PERFECT MATCH?	Penny Jordan
RED-HOT AND RECKLESS	Miranda Lee
BARGAIN WITH THE WIND	Kathleen O'Brien
THE DISOBEDIENT BRIDE	Elizabeth Power
ALL MALE	Kay Thorpe

Enchanted™

SANTA'S SPECIAL DELIVERY	Val Daniels
THE MARRIAGE PACT	Elizabeth Duke
A MIRACLE FOR CHRISTMAS	Grace Green
ACCIDENTAL WIFE	Day Leclaire
ONE NIGHT BEFORE CHRISTMAS	Catherine Leigh
A SINGULAR HONEYMOON	Leigh Michaels
A HUSBAND FOR CHRISTMAS	Emma Richmond
TEMPORARY GIRLFRIEND	Jessica Steele

MILLS & BOON®

The Season's Greetings Gift Pack brings you four fabulous romances from star-studded authors including Betty Neels.

And as an extra special Christmas treat we're offering the pack at a discounted price of just £6.60--that's 4 books for the price of 3.

The Mistletoe Kiss by Betty Neels
Merry Christmas by Emma Darcy
The Faithful Wife by Diana Hamilton
Home for Christmas by Ellen James

Available: November 1997

FREE!

FOUR FREE
specially selected
Enchanted™ novels
<u>PLUS</u> a FREE Mystery Gift
when you return this page...

Return this coupon and we'll send you 4 Mills & Boon® Romances from the Enchanted series and a mystery gift absolutely FREE! We'll even pay the postage and packing for you.

We're making you this offer to introduce you to the benefits of the Reader Service™– FREE home delivery of brand-new Mills & Boon Enchanted novels, at least a month before they are available in the shops, FREE gifts and a monthly Newsletter packed with information, competitions, author profiles and lots more...

Accepting these FREE books and gift places you under no obligation to buy, you may cancel at any time, even after receiving just your free shipment. Simply complete the coupon below and send it to:

MILLS & BOON READER SERVICE, FREEPOST, CROYDON, SURREY, CR9 3WZ.

READERS IN EIRE PLEASE SEND COUPON TO PO BOX 4546, DUBLIN 24

NO STAMP NEEDED

Yes, please send me 4 free Enchanted novels and a mystery gift. I understand that unless you hear from me, I will receive 6 superb new titles every month for just £2.20* each, postage and packing free. I am under no obligation to purchase any books and I may cancel or suspend my subscription at any time, but the free books and gift will be mine to keep in any case. (I am over 18 years of age)

N7YE

Ms/Mrs/Miss/Mr _____
BLOCK CAPS PLEASE

Address_____

_____

_____ Postcode _____

Offer closes 31st May 1998. We reserve the right to refuse an application. *Prices and terms subject to change without notice. Offer only valid in UK and Ireland and is not available to current subscribers to this series. Overseas readers please write for details.

You may be mailed with offers from other reputable companies as a result of this application. Please tick box if you would prefer not to receive such offers. ☐
Mills & Boon® is a registered trademark of Harlequin Mills & Boon Limited.

LaVyrle
SPENCER

The Hellion

Two Hearts…Worlds Apart

As teenagers they had shared a wild and reckless
love—and had been forced to pay the highest price.
Now, three broken marriages later, Tommy Lee Gentry
has come knocking on Rachel Hollis' door, begging
to be given another another chance.

*"LaVyrle Spencer has written a truly special story…The
Hellion is nostalgic and captures the feelings of love lost and
years wasted…SUPERB!"*

—Chicago Sun Times

Jennifer
BLAKE

GARDEN
of
SCANDAL

She wants her life back...

Branded a murderer, Laurel Bancroft has
been a recluse for years. Now she wants her
life back—but someone in her past will do
anything to ensure the truth stays buried.

*"Blake's style is as steamy as a still July
night...as overwhelmingly hot as Cajun spice."*
— Chicago Tribune

**AVAILABLE IN PAPERBACK
FROM NOVEMBER 1997**

GET TO KNOW
THE BEST OF ENEMIES

the latest blockbuster from TAYLOR SMITH

Who would you trust with your life? Think again.

*Linked to a terrorist bombing, a young student goes
missing. One woman believes in the girl's innocence
and is determined to find her before she is silenced.
Leya Nash has to decide—quickly—who to trust.
The wrong choice could be fatal.*

—

Valid only in the UK & Ireland against purchases made in retail outlets
and not in conjunction with any Reader Service or other offer.

50ᵖ OFF
COUPON
VALID UNTIL: 28.2.1998
TAYLOR SMITH'S *THE BEST OF ENEMIES*

To the Customer: This coupon can be used in part payment for a
copy of Taylor Smith's THE BEST OF ENEMIES. Only one coupon can
be used against each copy purchased. Valid only in the UK & Ireland
against purchases made in retail outlets and not in conjunction with
any Reader Service or other offer. Please do not attempt to redeem
this coupon against any other product as refusal to accept may cause
embarrassment and delay at the checkout.

To the Retailer: Harlequin Mills & Boon will redeem this coupon at
face value provided only that it has been taken in part payment for a
copy of Taylor Smith's THE BEST OF ENEMIES. The company reserves
the right to refuse payment against misredeemed coupons. Please
submit coupons to: Harlequin Mills & Boon Ltd. NCH Dept 730,
Corby, Northants NN17 1NN.

9 904170 200509 >

0472 00189